OSTAKIS

Angelica Primm

A NineStar Press Publication

Published by NineStar Press
P.O. Box 91792,
Albuquerque, New Mexico, 87199 USA.
www.ninestarpress.com

Ostakis

Printed in the USA
First Edition
February, 2019

Print ISBN: 978-1-950412-07-5

Also available in eBook, ISBN: 978-1-950412-03-7

Warning: This book contains sexually explicit content, which may only be suitable for mature readers.

Glossary of Terms at the end of the book.

The Human Planets Collective sent young Ambassador Kaj Deder to the former colony planet Ostakis to establish relations. But in the twenty-five hundred years since Earth lost contact with Ostakis, the people of that colony have dramatically changed. Kaj is tasked with finding the reason for these changes while he forges trade links between the HPC and Ostakis. Without trade with the HPC, the dwindling resources of Ostakis will ultimately end human life on the planet. But his mission faces a huge obstacle in the form of Most Reverend Thyenn Sharr, the head of the Faith Progressive Church, who sees the arrival of Kaj as the beginning of the end of the Church. Kaj's powerful attraction to Trademaster Klath's son, Arlan does not smooth relations.

Arlan Klath, the son of the Trademaster of Ostakis, bears the secret that the pious people of his planet want to hide from the homeworld and the HPC. The Curse of the Unspoken, wrought through the unspeakable acts of the First Colonists, afflicts all Ostakians, but some more strongly than others. Arlan is totally Cursed, considered born sinful and he lives without legal rights or property. He is scrutinized by Sharr who is enraged that Arlan's father defiantly refuses to submit Arlan to a cruel act to "redeem" Arlan's soul. The stakes increase when Arlan and Kaj form a relationship that Thyenn Sharr considers ample justification to usurp the Trademaster position through the power of his Church.

To S.B. who is still figuring things out and that's okay.

Chapter One

KAJ

Dearest Marta,

You would ask if I'm upset with my new posting. No. Not that. Discomforted. Yes. That is the correct word. You know I am a man who likes his routines, the stuff that meshes you to the pleasurable aspects of living. A delicious cup of coffee in the morning. Grilled vegetables on the barbecue and a nice glass of wine on the terrace in the evening. Everyday things.

Where I head is not ordinary...

Landfall is the most dangerous part of the journey.

The transport shook and rattled as it descended to hit the atmosphere of Ostakis. Flames flared from the heat shield and now I know why the pilot told me to pull the shade on my seat window. It's terrifying watching the flames of friction ignited ionized gas shimmer outside the window and engulf the ship. To take my mind off my impending death I mulled over my last briefing with Director Kotel.

"HOW TERRAFORMED IS this planet?" I had asked the director. We both paged our copies of the sparse notes and reports on Ostakis on our government issued readers. Survey had just turned in the information, and I was eager to see it. But, at the director's request, I had to wait until this meeting to go through it thoroughly.

"Not quite Earth normal," said Director Kotal. "Ten percent of the original plant and animal forms still survive. The Ostakians fight the planet's encroaching desert sands. The shield wall the colonists built is in disrepair."

That was an interesting bit of information. "Any reason why?"

"Our survey found abandoned population centers. Grey and Jacobs in Analysis think the number of people is shrinking. They may not have the workers to maintain it."

"So, after all this time, it has begun."

"Yes. It had to, didn't it?" She stood and stared out of the port window that revealed the desert planet beneath us. "If any planet needs what the HPC offers, it is Ostakis."

A silence hung between us. The urgency of the mission weighed more heavily.

"And another thing," she said. "The scout team reported rumors, or myths, of aboriginal tribes hiding in the desert."

We looked each other in the eye. The first hope of Earth had been finding indigenous sentients, but to our disappointment found none.

"Our lack of knowledge of the basis of the Faith Progressive Church hampers us. They didn't send literature on their precepts."

"Odd. Religions like to proselytize."

"Exactly. So we can only assume that there are things they don't want us to know. Be careful of Thyenn Sharr, Kaj. He's the church's head man. I can't impress this enough on you. Their highly conservative religious movement does not condone much that isn't praying and preaching. The hardest part of this assignment is conforming to the societal norms of the planet."

"Until I otherwise need to."

"Yes," she said with a nod of her head. "Until that. So tread carefully."

THE TRANSPORT LANDED screaming with a hard jolt and the increased gravity gripped my body, and the heat of the planet sucked my strength. The overheated air danced in shimmers off the newly built tarmac. Even terraforming didn't change the lack of humidity of this desert world circling a white sun. I took the steps of the high ladder of the flyer to the ground as if I were an old man. My joints groaned, and my lungs couldn't breathe. My section chief briefed me on the effects of a weightier g-force, but the reality jolted me. However, I had a job to complete, come calamity, storm, or the ache in my bones. The HPC, the Human Planets Collective, brought me to Ostakis to do it, and I thought I was ready.

I should have spent more time in the gym.

By the end of the descent, I sympathized with my grandfather much more, who always told me that aging hurts. As he predicted, so does a planet with a gravity 1.45 of Earth's. "That's nearly a half gee more," the old man had chuckled. He worked the space docks all his life and acclimated to adapting to different specific gravities. "You won't feel so spry then."

Thanks for your sage words, Gramps.

My welcoming committee stood in line solemnly at the bottom of the steps. Humans all, though a hundred generations removed from the main stock on Earth. We did not know what adaptations their bodies made to this world in the interval after Earth and her colonies lost contact. Now, aside from a scouting party gone horribly wrong, we were seeing each other for the first time in twenty-five centuries. None of us knew what to expect.

At the bottom of the high stair stood three men and a woman. One was dressed in robes reminiscent of old Earth clerics in black and white, and I assumed this was Thyenn Sharr. Another was an older silver-haired man dressed in what were formal street clothes, an all-body drape of cream fabric. The garment was unlike clothing I'd seen. It was a cross between a Roman toga and a kilt, though the Ostakians did not expose their skin. They accomplished this with a sheath of wide ribbons that covered their frame. Both the over and under cloth sported the pearly sheen reminiscent of superb Earth silk.

The third, a middle-aged gentleman, donned the same clothing. I recognized him from the dossier—Mar Seyatt, the mayor of Kiji Ost, the capital city of Ostakis. The lady attired herself in a provocative red wrap with a yellow under wrap. Her raven colored hair was piled on her head in a spiral. They all wore sandals.

The woman moved forward and bowed. "My house welcomes yours, Ambassador Deder," she said in the standard Ostakian greeting.

She mispronounced my name, a common enough error among non-Earth English speakers. "Forgive me. It's spoken as 'Deeder,' with a long *e*."

She nodded. "Please forgive my house for any offense."

"I took none," I assured her.

"Thank you, Ambassador Deder. I am Irdrana Vos, your counterpart from my government's side."

Ah. The first real slap in the face. The scouting expedition had discovered that women held a lesser status than men. Did someone mean her appointment as my equal as an insult? But she was lovely to look on, and I did not mind. I would make the best of it by ignoring their insult. They could laugh at me if they wished, whisper snide comments aside to each other, but there were worse things than working with an alluring woman.

It was evident she wanted this posting, though. She practiced her English so that barest hint of an accent graced her words. This was a small miracle as Ostakian gained many strange permutations of inflection that baffled Earth linguists.

I smiled graciously. "One of many I hope we share."

My reply deviated from standard conversational forms. A slight upturn of my counterpart's lips and her eyes' merriment told me she understood the game I played. She caught that I poked and prodded in the smallest of ways, testing the sincerity of the greeting I received. I might be young, but I was an ambassador's son. I'd watched my father on similar occasions many times.

Irdrana Vos was charming, yet professional, displaying the traits of the perfect ambassador. I hoped she found comparable qualities in me.

"And these are citizens you will interact with." Was her English not nuanced enough to know this was not the correct word? Or did she understand the differences in the shades of meaning and used it deliberately? "This is Most Reverend Thyenn Sharr, the high priest of the Faith Progressive Church."

I bowed as previously instructed and offered the standard greeting to a cleric.

"Faith and devotion always inspire hope," I replied in my rudimentary Ostakian. I prayed, but not to some incorporeal godhead, that I would get this right. Sharr was not a man to offend. Ostakis sent its language manuals later than we requested. I jammed in what my poor brain could pick up while we waited for them to construct the spaceport. Hopefully, I would learn the rest quickly.

"Why thank you, Mr. Deder," he said with the barest of smiles. Irdrana shot him a vexed glance. It did not escape me he refused to use my title nor offer me a similarly standard greeting. *Okay, then. Not a fan.*

"And the Trademaster of Ostakis, Aulkus Klath."

"We welcome your house to ours," said Klath. He didn't speak warmly, but at least he used the correct words. He was cautious, but not unfriendly.

I bowed once again. "My house rejoices in your welcome." The Trademaster betrayed the barest of smiles. So, this was a man who appreciates niceties.

"And the mayor of Kiji Ost, Mar Seyatt."

I bowed again. "My house begs your indulgence to join your city." It was an awkward sequence of words in English, but in Ostakian the correct form.

Seyatt broke into the first smile I received that day, and I instantly distrusted him. That grin was odd, unnaturally wide, and unsettling.

"It's a pleasure to meet you," he replied enthusiastically in an Earth-style fashion. Ah, a xenophile. Or pretending to be one. That put me in a culturally awkward position. Not only did Seyatt ignore my traditional plea for acceptance, making me entirely unwelcome in the city he lorded, he expected me to greet him as an old friend. It was pointedly impolite. I noticed Sharr's lips curl in a self-satisfied half scowl at my upcoming humiliation, while Irdrana's expression communicated she wanted to harm Seyatt. Klath stood the farthest from me of the three, his face drawn tight in discomfort at the imminent cultural debacle.

The microseconds ticked while I formed a response that fulfilled forms that did not make me appear an uncultured fool parroting words without understanding their meaning. The sweat beading my brow was not due to the heat. But why not play on assumptions?

"My house welcomes your friendship."

I was playing with fire. With those words, I called Seyatt on prematurely acting a friend when we had not yet established trust between us. And I did so politely. He now had two choices. Seyatt could stand by the inferred offer, which could prove difficult for him if I failed my mission or walk it back. That would embarrass him and his house.

Seyatt's face lost color. In front of these observers, my reply shoved my foot inside Ostakian society. By this planet's laws, witnesses trumped a written record, photograph, or video. Now Seyatt could not gainsay my supposal. But he was the person who acted in an overly friendly manner. Any Ostakian would assume the honor of an offered friendship, so I would too.

Irdrana's eyes brimmed with merriment while Klath's lips upturned in the barest of smiles. Sharr's expression grew hard as he stared at me like a monster that threatened to devour all of them. Seyatt stood there, silent, not knowing how to respond, and the tension thickened.

Klath coughed, breaking the unease, and all heads turned to the trademaster.

"Shall we retire to my home for daymeal?" he offered. It was an incredibly polite offer. Ostakians reserved daymeals for family, friends, and close business associates. Within minutes of my arrival, I had jetted into a new social position within Ostakian society.

Beginner's luck, I warned myself.

I contemplated the three of them. Irdrana had an unnatural arch to the curve of her dark brow, and Klath an undertone of orange to his skin not seen on earth. Detecting a difference in Sharr was hard. Cleric clothing covered everything but his face. What aberration did he hide under his clothes? Seyatt looked entirely human except that extra-wide smile. Something happened in the genetics of the people here that did not follow the typical path of evolution. The First Contact teams suspected that, and one of my jobs was to find out if it were true.

Would it please the cautious Kotal that I jammed my foot into the social structure of Ostakis within my first moments of arrival? Or would she think I moved too quickly?

But haste in all forms chased this operation. There was much to accomplish before the HPC cruiser hiding in orbit around Ostakis' moon left for another former Earth colony. Either I stayed or left with that ship after I performed any of my assignments, the first being evaluating whether Ostakian society could fit within the HPC framework. My superiors' current thinking was that it did not. How Ostakis received me was the first test.

I followed my welcoming committee and stepped off the concrete onto crushed gravel. This spaceport was brand new, erected on the hope of Ostakis entering the Human Planet Collective and establishing trade with member worlds. But it was incomplete. The mission commander patiently waited as the Ostakians built the required landing space for off-world transport. But the ship that delivered me had a tight schedule and other places to go. We could not wait for them to finish construction. As soon as the natives laid the tarmac, my people sent me in the flyer.

I looked over the shoulders of the welcoming committee to the city that lay at the edge of the spaceport.

It was a long walk, even for me who was used to walking everywhere. And the gravity and the heat rapidly claimed me as its victim as we made for the brand new Ostakian terminal. Fresh paint greeted my nose, and I spotted no security personnel at the gate. When two electric vehicles that reminded me of golf carts arrived, I gratefully took the seat Irdrana Vos offered. Soon we entered the city proper, and I marveled as we rolled along streets as straight as a ruler. A few modest gleaming and newly built skyscrapers dominated the streetscape. Seyatt, playing tour guide, kept a running commentary of the accomplishments of Ostakis.

The whir of the electric engine stymied conversation. We lurched side to side as the driver zig-zagged erratically to avoid pedestrians. The driver's efforts earned us curious and impolite stares as we whizzed past the people of Kiji Ost. I could imagine their dialogue.

That's him, the man from Earth.

Tsk, don't you have anything to do other than gossip?

His skin is as pale as the night moon.

He comes from the stars, doesn't he?

The wheels of the electric vehicle jolted onto uneven cobbles in an older part of the city. The streets narrowed, shutting out the sun. People pressed close together traveling on their daily routines. Modern and old, wide and close, bright and dark, these were the contrasts of my new home.

In which light would I stand in the coming days? Despite the heat, I shivered, because I did not know the answer.

Chapter Two

ARLAN

Ija, our cook, frantically rushed from one dish to another. That didn't stop her from batting my hand when I reached for an appetizer from a tray recently pulled from the oven.

"Away!" she snapped.

The back door opened and my best friend Pib strolled in and zeroed in on the pastry puffs on the counter.

"Out, you reprobates!" Ija shrieked.

Pib scored a handful of pastries and smiled as Ija snapped kitchen towels at us. We scuttled from the cookroom like the domestic thieves we were.

"Are you going to share the wealth?" I asked.

Pib snorted. "Hah! Just because I was faster than you."

"I didn't want to earn the wrath of my father. Ija tattles."

"What is her dysfunction this morning?"

"Father is bringing the Earth Ambassador to daymeal."

"What?" Pib's mouth opened, full of a half-eaten puff. "How did that happen?"

I shrugged my shoulders. "A messenger showed up ten minutes ago, and Ija has been frantic since."

"Will he allow you to sit at daymeal?"

"Why wouldn't he?" I asked with an indignant huff.

For once Pib stood speechless.

"Am I not," I said, hammering home my point, "a worthy representative of House Klath?"

"Oh hell, Arlan," he said. "I didn't mean—"

I let Pib stumble. Prejudice ran rampant among us for those like me and Pib, who bore the Curse of the Unspoken, but my father and others worked to correct that. Unlike many heads of households, my father educated me, and I now enjoyed a crucial place in the business of the Trademaster of Ostakis. My natural head for numbers, one of the legacies of the Cursed, positioned me as my father's primary accountant. I had even, with his permission, secured work with other families in the same capacity, and I refused to live my life in the shadows.

Pib, however, was not as lucky. His family insisted on treating him like the horror most of our society did our kind. That was why Pib spent more time here than at his own home. To entertain him while I worked, I tutored him in my trade and gave him small pieces of work. I wanted to do more for my best friend, but the law was the law, and Father could not employ Pib in regular service without his family's permission. Of course, the thought horrified them.

We walked back to my office, but Pib stayed curiously quiet. When we entered the bookcase-lined room, filled with hundreds of years of Klath ledgers, Pib sat at his desk with an angered huff.

"What is it, Pib?" I asked. It was unlike the usually jovial Pib to be this silent. "I'm sorry I gave you a difficult time."

His face twisted. "It's not you, Arlan. It's my family."

I waited. I suffered along with Pib the various indignities they heaped upon him.

"They've arranged a partnership for me!"

Partnership. What a euphemism. Under our laws, it was domestic slavery.

"What?"

"Far to the North in Kiji Amst."

My heart dropped to my stomach as the horrifying realization ran through my bones. Pib's family intended to send him so far away I might not see him again. "No."

"It's worse."

"How?"

"He has a wife."

"Oh." That was horrible news.

"Any children we have, unless they were like me, would be clanless."

He didn't have to say it. For Pib's sake, I tried to keep standing at this devastating news. Nothing was more important than House and Clan, and for his family to so heartlessly condemn their future grandchildren to clanlessness was beyond cruel. But they wouldn't see it that way.

"They can't do this," I declared.

"Can't they?" he asked bitterly. "It's that, or they disown me. They want me out of the house, Arlan, and there is nothing I can do about it."

"You'll stay here." I spoke brashly in my outrage.

"As what? A beggar?"

"No, not that, Pib. Never that. You are as dear as a son to my father. He won't let this happen."

"That's a fool's dream, Arlan. Even the Trademaster of Ostakis can't gainsay the law."

"I'll ask him to buy out the partnership contract and use my own money."

Pib's eyes flashed a brief second of hope, but it died quickly.

"Arlan," he said. And then he turned his head away so I didn't witness his tears. "You are the best friend any man can have. But they don't want me because I am the reminder of their shame."

"That's Thyenn Sharr talking, Pib."

"Arlan," boomed my father through the house. His voice was a hearty baritone, but more than that, he projected it for maximum effect.

I put my hand on Pib's shoulder, regretful I had to leave him. "Stay. I'll ask Ija to bring you daymeal. And some sums need work." I handed him a ledger. "The receipts and notes are inside."

"No, Arlan. This is one of your most important clients."

"Arlan?" called my father again. His voice shook the entrance to the family offices. I did not have time to talk about this more. There were worse things than keeping your friend from running off by offering tempting labor he hadn't done before.

"You can do this. I trust you. Now, my father calls."

"Go," said Pib. He clutched the account book to his chest, and the gratitude in his eyes singed my heart. It was such a small thing, this work, and just because we were Cursed, we shouldn't be grateful doing it.

"Sorry, Father," I called as I scrambled from my room to meet him.

But in my haste, I stumbled on the threshold of my office and fell forward. Father steadied me with his strong arms, but when I looked up, I met the crystal blue eyes of the whitest man I'd ever seen.

His coloring shocked me. His complexion was so pale it did not even appear pink. His hair, close-cropped and brushed back, was the barest of yellow-brown. And he was tall, towering over my father by at least a head—and Aulkus Klath stood above most men. But those eyes. They were an ice blue that glittered with amusement and intelligence. They drew me as surely as a compass pointed north. My breath stuttered in my chest.

"Easy there, boy," said my father. He smiled indulgently. And for that, I was forever grateful. He did not care I was Cursed. "And this is my son, Arlan Klath. Arlan, this is the Earth ambassador, Kaj Deter."

What was my father doing? Why did he bring this stranger into the familiar part of the house, and without the rest of the day meal guests? I stood like an idiot, unable to breathe. Words thickened in my throat as my heart beat faster. Oh no. This was impossible. My father introduced me to one of the most influential men on the planet, and I stood besotted and useless. At that moment I was truly Cursed.

The ambassador bowed as if I were a person of importance, which was gracious. And wrong.

"My house," he said in stumbling Ostakian, "is honored in meeting you."

Oh damn. We couldn't mislead the man about where I fit in the social structure, could we? I shot a glance at my father, who smiled warmly.

"There is no honor necessary, Ambassador Deder. You are as welcome in my abode as any family member."

In a flash, I understood what my father was doing. In introducing me separately of a formal gathering, he intended to make Earth's diplomat a de facto relative. He now bound the man into loyalty to House Klath. It was reckless. We did not know the man's character or his intentions. Either this was the most brilliant move my father ever made, or the most disastrous.

The emissary was no fool. Confusion filled those startling blue eyes for a moment. But only just, and he turned it off like blowing out a candle.

"Your words," said Deder, "are honeyed treasures to a weary traveler."

Oh, gods. Could he be more elegant? In one phrase he took the offer of friendship but cautioned that he was an interloper and might not be able to fulfill the duties of such a contract. Who would have thought to pull out that old chestnut of a greeting form and make it work at this moment?

"Your road has indeed been long," said my father with a smile. He acted the most gracious I had ever seen him. The subtext of his words conveyed that he would take no offense if Deder could not fulfill his obligations of friendship.

While I loved my father, he could be imperious and demanding, and more than one challenger died under his sword for breaches of honor against our House. All knew this about Aulkus Klath except this outworlder, who took his life in his hands by accepting fellowship from House Klath. And now the Trademaster of Ostakis in a single sentence absolved him of any future wrong against us.

I doubted this foreigner recognized what just passed. And who knew if the courts would consider me, a Cursed, a reliable witness to this exchange. But when my father's eyes met the Earth ambassador's, there was something I had not seen there in a long time.

It was trust.

Did Kaj Deder know the gift my father gave him?

Chapter Three

KAJ

Dearest Marta,

What would you say when I left you to come to this place? Left you behind on the beautiful blue pearl in the sea of stars that is an awe to behold but a danger to touch? You'd hate me and be right to. We knew in University that our jobs could separate us.

Now millions of miles separate you and me, and I cannot visit you despite my ardent desire. But the distance does not heal the hole in my heart. The work does not cauterize the breach of our separation. The parsecs between your body and mine only leaves me singular and alone, and I cannot help but yearn for you.

Such impossible thoughts.

I was out of my depth. What had happened when Aulkus Klath dragged me along to "gather" his son from his work? The patriarch was no doubt a doting father as he chatted about his son as we made our way through the winding hallways of the residence.

We had left the welcoming committee in the atrium as servants ushered them into the dining room. Thyenn Sharr frowned over his shoulder as Klath insisted on giving me a tour of his house.

"Enjoy the honor," murmured Irdrana under her breath as I squeezed past her as Klath urgently waved me over. She had stepped forward as if she expected the same offer, but Klath did not make it. Casually, as if I were an old friend from college recently arrived, Klath led me through his house, mentioning bits of family history surrounding different possessions.

House Klath was a large dwelling filled with winding wood-paneled hallways and many rooms. In a way, it was distinctly not human. Humans loved order, straight lines, and large, empty spaces so we could see our enemies coming. This was not a place of enemies, but family, tumbling upon each other in familial closeness. If left to my own devices, I would lose my way.

We arrived in a section of the house where the lines straightened.

"These are the main offices of my business," said Klath. "Of course, I do have offices in each of the major cities of Ostakis. But this is the heart of my business. Arlan," he boomed, loud enough to rattle pictures on the wall nearest us.

"My son," he continued with evident pride, "is my head accountant. I could not keep my business in order without his assistance. Last year, he found a huge discrepancy in the sums transferred in a business deal with a trader from Kiji Amst. Very disagreeable people. The trader claimed we misunderstood the currency exchange rate, but Arlan proved him wrong. And in court too." He spoke the last words with immeasurable pride.

"Arlan," he called again, and this time a young man stumbled from a doorway and pitched forward into his father's arms, murmuring apologies. Despite his nut-brown skin, a blush spread across his cheeks and throat, causing my breath to hitch. Even for an Ostakian, he was small and slim, though not skinny. The muscles of his arms bunched under his tight tunic. His fey Ostakian eyes caught the faint light in the hallway, reflecting shards of glittering gold as his face turned up to meet my gaze.

Aulkus righted the young man easily. Arlan's gleaming dark hair was twisted into a tight bun. My mind strayed most inappropriately to pulling it apart and watching his hair tumble to his shoulders.

I have a weakness for men with long hair. Women too. But on men, it is so much more unexpected.

"And this is my son, Arlan Klath," said the elder Klath. "Arlan, this is the Earth ambassador, Kaj Deder."

"My house," I said, hoping I got the conjugation correct, "is honored in meeting you."

Confusion washed over the young man's face, and I wondered if I said something wrong. He looked to his father, who only smiled.

"There is no honor necessary, Ambassador Deder. You are as welcome in my house as any family member."

What? But something in the elder Klath's words sparked a revelation in Arlan's beautiful face. Apparently, I was now considered a member of the family? This was strange and wrong, like trying to kiss a woman too quickly on a first date. My brain furiously dug through the ritualized forms to come up with the proper response and found one, though even to my mind it sounded archaic.

"Your words," I said, "are honeyed treasures to a weary traveler."

What I meant was, "I don't know what's happening here, so please forgive me if I make mistakes."

Klath smiled even more broadly, and the younger Klath's face relaxed into understanding. I grinned, too, hiding my discomfort.

The three of us returned to the atrium, whose ordered symmetry now shouted new meaning. It was an enormous space where you could gather fifty people and not crowd them. The roof was a high dome with five rafters of curved dark wood that met in the middle to form a five-pointed star. The beams ran down the walls to join the polished white stone floor. This was the place of ritual and formal greeting, of a space large enough to see your enemies coming.

Between two of the ribs on the left-hand side, a dark wood double door opened revealing the large formal dining room. We entered with the younger Klath two paces behind us. The place settings sat at one end of the table that seated fifty, and my mind flashed disjointedly to the symbolism of that number. Fifty was the number of heroes who followed the Greek Jason on that quest, and who suffered for their loyalty to him. But the bible names fifty as the number of joy and the feast. Others consider it the holiest of integers because it equals to the sum of the square numbers $9 + 16 + 25$ constructed on the sacred triangle of Pythagoras. Twenty-five hundred years later, did the Ostakians remember any of this, or was this an instinctual heuristic manifestation of their Earth heritage?

"Please sit," boomed Klath. He moved to the head of the table, and Arlan sat to his left while he waved me to the seat of honor at his right side. He pulled on a thick cord behind him.

"Ambassador Vos, would you sit by Arlan here, and Most Reverend Sharr, by our honored guest, and of course, Mayor Seyatt, by our holy guest. Thank you."

Not exactly boy, girl, boy, girl, I thought. But what did I expect in a pointedly patriarchal society?

"This is a beautiful table. Is this mahogany?" I asked with wonder. On the Earth on which I grew up such things were rare, and I only knew what wood it was because of my father. One of his postings was at the Embassy in Old London, which managed to save their ancient furnishings from the uprisings.

"Yes. The colonial Klaths brought it from Earth."

The extra cartage fees must have cost them a fortune. So the Klaths always had money to drag along an otherwise useless thing on a colony expedition.

The servants brought in the first round, plates of small foods that seemed like appetizers. I drew out the food analyzer in my pocket and held it for Klath's inspection.

"Good host," I said. "This device measures whether I can eat this food. I mean no offense in its use."

"You find such things, necessary?" asked Seyatt. He seemed surprised.

"It is a different world for the ambassador," affirmed Irdrana. "If you remember the early settlers had many problems with sickness. And our scientists theorized that may have been from foreign substances in the foods, things to which we adapted. Ambassador, has such a thing been found on other colony worlds?"

I took a sip of wine to buy time while forming my answer. Protocol told me I was not to discuss other colonies at this early stage. But withholding information could damage the fragile trust growing between us.

"The basis of life remains constant throughout the galaxy. However, different planets developed varying mixes of enzymes and minerals. Those that stray too far from the narrow band of human needs prove uninhabitable."

There. I clued these people on the problem we discovered in Ostakis' original colonization surveys. Ostakis was an imperfect colony planet. It lacked important metals and minerals needed for self-sustained technological growth. This deficiency also affected the quality and quantity of crops. The first reports of the thriving population on Ostakis surprised us.

In the frenzy to colonize as many planets as possible, the planning teams allowed shortcuts. They believed the planet contained enough nutrient rich minerals to carry the planet through the first stages of colonization. Three or four generations may have survived such conditions. Not one hundred. I was looking at people who shouldn't exist.

Seyatt cocked his head in thought. "Fascinating," he said dryly. "I suppose I am lucky he and the others at this table are not scientists who would demand a more thorough explanation of my words." He tipped his wine glass.

"Thank you. It is the summer wine from three seasons ago. It's just turned drinkable."

"So, you are a vintner?" I asked.

"My family's business was winemaking," replied Klath. "I inherited it when my father passed. But that was long after I took up the Trademaster position when I partnered with Arlan's birthparent."

I looked up from my food inspection. "Pardon?" The word birthparent confused me.

"Simply," said Irdrana with a scowl at the Trademaster. "When Aulkus joined the Clan Klath he brought his inheritance with him. The Trademaster's original last name was Wren."

"Is that usual to change one's name when marrying into another clan?" *There is something I'm not grasping here, and I can't put my finger on it.*

"Only certain families," said Seyatt.

"On Old Earth, we had royal families and when a male of a lower status married into a higher status, he sometimes adopted the name of the higher status family. Is it like that?"

Sharr made a rude noise in his throat. Irdrana ignored him and smiled at me.

"Something like that," said Irdrana.

I'd finished my inspection of the food, and the delicate sensors found nothing that would poison me. I reached for a pastry wrapped puff when Sharr cleared his throat.

"Klath?" asked Sharr.

"Yes?" The elder Klath took a sip of his wine as his eyes glittered with amusement. The younger Klath looked as if he would shrink in his seat from embarrassment. Was Klath playing a game with the cleric?

"Should we not have a prayer for the meal?" asked Sharr.

"Ah, yes. I was so engrossed in our conversation I forgot we had not offered one. Ambassador, would you care to proffer a food dedication from your world?"

Sharr's face turned beet red, but he was a guest, and could not protest further. From the daggers in his eyes, he would have killed me given a chance.

"Is that appropriate?" I asked. "I'm not sure of your forms in this matter." There was no religious matter in the language texts the Ostakians had sent, which was odd. I didn't want to step on any clerical toes, and Sharr looked as if I couldn't avoid stubbing them.

"We all spring from the same source," said Klath as if reciting a religious verse. "I'm sure we can tolerate a simple prayer from the homeworld, can't we, Reverend Sharr?"

"I would be interested to hear it," said Sharr flatly. His frown demonstrated he was unhappy with this intrusion into his field of expertise, but I couldn't insult my host either.

"Here it goes then." I clasped my hands and bent my head. "Bless us, oh Lord, these thy gifts, from your bounty. Amen."

"Well," said Seyatt, "that was sweetly brief. Can't wait to get to your meal, eh?"

"Something like that," I replied.

Klath cleared his throat. "I appreciate a short prayer. Some food dedications let the food grow cold."

Irdrana chuckled, and Sharr looked as if he'd do violence.

Klath snapped his fingers at a servant waiting discretely by the wall for orders.

"Refill the wine glasses," he said. "In fact, fill them as needed."

I watched this exchange with interest because it revealed much about this society. The servant didn't move unless ordered to do so. This was Ostakis then.

The servant nodded and freshened the wine around the table. I started on my second glass but immediately regretted it. The over-strong wine hit me like a tsunami rolling in one inexorable wave.

At my incipient intoxication, I reminded myself to keep a clear head and set the wine glass on the table.

The second course arrived, a slab of meat, but from what animal I did not know. I stared at it, not knowing what to say. I ate a vegetarian diet, as most people from Earth did.

"Forgive me," I said quietly to Klath. "I cannot eat this."

"Oh," he said with consternation. "I am sorry."

"No need to apologize. You are a gracious host."

"You do not consume meat?" asked Arlan.

"We are a world of thirteen billion," I said carelessly, and Sharr's eyes widened. "We devote our resources to agriculture. Raising meat has a negative feed to output ratio—" I stopped in the middle of my speech to see all at the table staring at me.

"Thirteen billion?" Sharr's voice became shrill. "What prevents you from bringing your greater numbers here and taking our planet from us?"

Now it was my turn to stare. "Why would we do that?" I asked stupidly.

Then I realized my clumsiness and idiocy. The wine must have hit me harder than I thought. I mindlessly told these Ostakians that in the scheme of things they were not significant enough to take by force. Which was true.

But a diplomat's job was to pave and maintain smooth relations with our assigned nation. It was our duty to treat our charges with utmost respect and their interests with importance.

I was at the cusp of failing my diplomatic mission.

Chapter Four

ARLAN

I did not think the Earth Ambassador could get any paler, but I was wrong. As the blood drained from his face, his skin turned a light shade of blue. Did he have a bad reaction to the wine? The food? Or the pointed and rude hostility of Thyenn Sharr?

My father's face held a curious mixture of shock and amusement. If he meant to shake things up, he accomplished his mission. But I felt sorry for the Earth ambassador. He stepped into a pile of excrement waiting for his footsteps. It did not matter if it was this incident or another. Thyenn Sharr planned to make this man into a demon, and he did not deserve it.

"Surely you came to establish trade with us, Ambassador?" I asked.

Deder blinked. "Yes. That is our first mission here."

"My son is right," said Aulkus. "We should start with a small one, eh? To test the waters?"

Deder looked at me, and his eyes held mine with a new appreciation for righting this daymeal to its correct course.

"That's been the plan all along," he said.

"Excellent," said my father. "What do you propose to trade?"

"We'd like to start with a cultural exchange. Of classic literature, perhaps?"

"Stories?" I asked. That was a curious exchange, but I saw where giving the people of Ostakis a window into the minds of the homeworld would groom smoother relations between them and us.

"I think that is an excellent start," said Irdrana. "Will you be translating the works into Ostakian?"

"Yes," he said. "We've already completed the work."

"How?" I asked, astonished. "That seems a tremendous feat."

"We've done this many times. Once you delivered the manuals for your language, we uploaded them into our databanks and made machine translations of the text. Then a team of linguistic experts who studied the manuals combed through the translations to make sure we captured the original intent of the language accurately into yours. Since the manuals arrived late, I received the electronic copies en route. I'm authorized to contract a printer to produce hard copies."

"That seems incredible," said Mar Seyatt. "When you say you've done this many times, how many is that?"

"We've re-established contact with two hundred different colony worlds within the past two decades, Earth time. We have hundreds more to go."

"Two hundred?" Irdrana whispered.

"We want nothing more than to bring all humans into the Human Planets Collective. Each member world we induct adds to our strength."

"And puts all others under the same thumb," declared Sharr.

"No," said Deder with a frown. "We are a representative collective. Should your planet join, you will add your voice to the Collective. If you don't, well, then there is always trade if you wish it."

"And if we don't?" snarled Sharr.

"Then we leave you alone."

"Are you saying that there is nothing we have of value to your Collective?" asked Irdrana.

My cousin was unusually perceptive. That she drew this observation out of the conversation amazed me. But she was correct in her assessment, and she uncovered the danger to Ostakis in this exchange.

The ambassador recognized it, too. Deder sat straighter in his chair and leveled his gaze at her.

"I meant no disrespect," he replied. "Our First Contact teams, aside from a few oddities, found nothing remarkable about Ostakis."

Defeat hung about his words, and my heart went out to him. Deder's words were utterly honest yet revealed so much. It was Ostakis that would benefit most from contact with the Collective, and we had nothing to leverage a better position. I had watched my father often enough with businessmen who were not his equal. He treated them with great respect, which was why they loved him. He never sent a man from his table or meeting room feeling as if he had nothing of worth to give.

Deder had just spent all his currency with the movers and shakers of Ostakis. If he were not careful, Ostakis would regard him as a great fool sent on a mission a robot could have accomplished.

"I think you are wrong in that," said Sharr.

Deder glanced at Sharr with a neutral expression, but his eye betrayed amusement. "Oh?"

"We have antiquities of the Faith Progressive Church such as items from the First Landing. Would these things interest you?"

Deder shot the cleric a most charming grin, and even I with my untutored eye saw it as an ambassadorial tool meant to disarm.

"Of course. We are supremely interested in Ostakian history."

"Good," said Sharr. "If you want to trade literature, we'll exchange pieces of our holy history for them. And we will see how the truth shakes out."

If Sharr were not so powerful, my father would consider him an idiot. He was a demagogue whose words held sway over many Ostakian hearts. The problem with Sharr, as with most men of unquestioning faith, was he believed the words he spouted. And that, as my father reminded me many times, was what made him dangerous.

Deder smiled again. "Why certainly, Most Reverend Sharr. That sounds like the perfect exchange."

Irdrana and Seyatt murmured their assent, but my father merely nodded. Everyone but the ambassador knew the church considered antiquities before the Curse clean and unsullied, holy in that way, but not valuable. No, value rested in artifacts and words that came from when we realized the Unspoken cursed us, and our path toward Enlightenment began. The proposed exchange was ironic. Sharr traded things of no value for what he would declare from the pulpit of no use to Ostakis.

A slight, wry upturn of my father's lips told me what he thought of that. However, no one on Ostakis was in a position to gainsay Most Reverend Thyenn Sharr. Father called for more wine to mellow our guests, and the conversation turned to less controversial subjects. At least I thought so.

"So tell us about your family," said Irdrana. "Do you have a wife?"

Deder twirled the stem of his wineglass in his long, supple fingers and then set it down. The ping of the crystal on the wood table seemed to punctuate his hidden thoughts. The Ambassador knitted his brows as his discomfort rolled off him. "No," he mumbled.

"Oh, sorry to hear," said Irdrana. "Marriage is a blessing." She fell silent then but we all wanted to hear more. Here on Ostakis a man his age would be engaged or contracted, but apparently that was not an Earth custom.

"I suppose," he sighed, and then glanced at the inquisitive eyes watching him.

"How do people on Earth make marriages?" asked Irdrana. Her curiosity overcame her good sense.

Kaj scrunched his brow and tightened his jaw. "Excuse me?"

"Here, families arrange marriages or partnerships when young people come of age."

"I see. Arlan, are you engaged?" Kaj turned the beacon of his bright blue eyes toward me. I blushed at being addressed directly. His question revealed his lack of understanding of my situation. But how can he know? Thyenn Sharr made it clear we weren't to discuss the sinners among us.

"No, I am contracted to partner with an associate of my father's."

"I'm sorry," Kaj said. "I don't understand."

Thyenn Sharr glanced at me with disapproval before turning his attention to the ambassador. "Men, like Arlan, are not allowed the sacred sacrament of marriage. They lead men to sin, as the Trademaster well knows."

My father glared at Sharr. I shifted uncomfortably in my seat. This was an old argument between them, as my father put aside his wife to partner with my birthparent.

House Klath weathered the scandal. But Sharr had publicly declared my birthparent Segun's death in childbirth with his second child God's retribution for Segun's sin. My father never forgave Sharr that sermon from his pulpit. This disastrous conversation threatened to end the evening on a sour note.

Kaj must have picked up on it because he suddenly shifted the conversation. "You should be glad for whatever relationships you have. They are all dead, the people I knew."

We all stared at him and I wondered at his point.

"How horrible," said Irdrana.

"No," he said. "It is physics. Ostakis is four hundred light years from earth. It takes that long for one particle of light to travel from Earth to here. Ship time took two years, using Earth time as a measure. But because of what the scientists call time dilation five hundred years passed on Earth before I arrived. I am sorry I am not a physicist who can explain it better."

All around the table gaped at him.

"You left your family and friends behind to come here knowing you could never see them again?" asked Irdrana. There was awe in her voice. "Why would you do that?"

"Because we have at least three hundred more colonies to visit before we've completed the task of unifying humanity."

A silence settled over the table. Sharr continued to glare at Kaj, who stumbled on in wine slurred words.

"It is important work. As recent events taught us, there are grave dangers setting foot on newly rediscovered worlds."

Kaj's words horrified me. Surely the ambassador was wine besotted, but he needed to have a care. All it took was a misplaced word, a cultural convention defied, and he might find himself at the end of someone's knife.

Like the first representatives of his people to this world.

Sharr cut enthusiastically into his steak. "Surely you cannot blame us for spies your people placed among us."

What was wrong with Sharr? He did not have the Ambassador's excuse of not knowing the strength of my father's wine. Did he think he'd score points by embarrassing the Ambassador in front of important people? Or did he hope to draw a Challenge out of Kaj Deder to provide the excuse for the Ambassador's death?

"But I only say these words because I am among friends." Kaj stared pointedly at Sharr just a hair's breadth short of hostile intent.

A flicker of alarm registered in my father's eyes. As host, it was his responsibility to make sure no violence crossed his threshold. He rightly gauged the Ambassador's level of intoxication. I watched in horror as this daymeal spun out of control yet again.

"You will forgive me if I consider the needs of my people first," said Sharr. "It is a dangerous thing to insert ignorant people into our society. I would not see the peace of Ostakis disturbed by unknown elements."

Now Seyatt and Irdrana's faces registered alarm.

"Most Reverend Sharr," started Irdrana. But Deder did not give her a chance to finish.

"I forgive everything, Most Reverend Sharr. Especially under the influence of Trademaster Klath's wine. It is"—he cast a look at each one at the table—"most delicious and most potent. I succumb to its influence."

He slurred his last words with a huge grin, and we all laughed, except Sharr. The tension in my father's shoulders released.

"I consider myself lucky then," said Sharr sarcastically.

Sharr, the fool, could not stop speaking. Was it his mission to humiliate the Ambassador? My father decided to mitigate this rapidly devolving situation.

"Arlan," said my father, "show the Ambassador to a guest room so he may rest from his long journey. Afterward, we will escort him to his residence."

"I don't want to be any trouble," Deder slurred.

"No trouble," said my father. "You should meet your staff in a more rested state, anyway. Arlan?"

"Yes, Father. Please follow me, Ambassador."

Deder stood and bowed. "It has been my great pleasure to meet you all."

He walked under my shoulder from the formal dining room, but as soon as we entered the main residence, he stumbled.

"Damn," he muttered. "That's some strong wine."

I offered my shoulder. "Here, I will help you."

"I'm sorry," Deder muttered.

His body pressed against mine and I found I liked it despite the fact he was drunk and acted halfway the fool. But his body was attractive, even if he didn't have the stocky Ostakian build. He smelled masculine, and my physical reaction embarrassed me.

But he seemed not to notice the stiffening in my pants or was too polite to mention it, which was refreshing. Some men often took delight in embarrassing a Cursed with their natural reactions to what was biology.

We finally reached the main guest room, one kept up daily by the servants, and I steered him inside.

"You are very strong," he murmured.

I led him to the bed. "Take your rest, Ambassador."

He sat and came face to face with my excitement. He reached for my arm and touched it gently. The soft trailing of his fingers down my limb sent tingles through me, and I bit my lip.

"You needn't leave," he said huskily as he gazed at me through half-lidded eyes.

I coughed to cover my growing excitement. Laying with this man was a very appealing thought. But, of course, impossible. "Thank you, for your kind offer, Ambassador. But as I said I am promised to another."

"Promised?" he asked stupidly, and I worried that somehow the wine poisoned him.

"In partnership."

"Oh," he said with a confused expression on his face. "Yes, you did say. My apologies."

He looked disappointed, which warmed my foolish heart. In my years I had found no man or woman attractive, which was why I consented to Ushos Phale's partnership offer. It would be a marriage of convenience. Ushos would satisfy the needs of my body while I fulfilled his desire to climb social and career ladders. At my age, the heats were becoming painful rather than annoying. The physician warned my father that if I didn't obtain a partner, I might die from the stress of them.

"No need to apologize," I said. "You didn't or wouldn't know."

"What do you mean?" he asked.

I couldn't explain more. Even our language denied the intimacy of partnerships. How could a man from an alien culture understand?

"Take your rest, Ambassador. My father will come for you in a few hours. By then the worst of the day's heat will have passed and you can travel the streets more safely."

"Arlan?" he asked as he swung his feet on the bed and lay back into the pillows.

"Yes?" I didn't protest the use of my first name. Yes, it was unseemly, but I felt very improper around this man.

"Call me Kaj."

Kaj. What a rare name. Sophisticated yet strong as if he could show rough edges. I liked it.

"As you wish, Kaj."

"Thank you, Arlan." His eyelids fluttered, and soon his breathing slowed. I stood like a fool watching him fall asleep, unable to tear myself away and not understanding why.

Only until he was finally under did I walk away quietly and pulled the door closed slowly so as not to make a noise. But what should I do now? Return to the meal or go back to work? If I did not go back to the dining room, that would give Sharr the occasion to misapprehend what happened between Kaj Deder and me. But returning would subject me to more of Sharr's snide comments, and in my present mood, I did not want to deal with them.

And then there was a distressed Pib in my office, working. I shouldn't leave him alone.

I decided to return but announced I had work to do. That would still give Sharr no bones to grind. But let him. It was no secret what I do for House Klath.

I must have been absent longer than I thought. When I returned to the dining room, Vos and Seyatt had left. And my father was in a heated discussion with Thyenn Sharr.

"The law used to be that the church spared a contracted or partnered Cursed, and my son is contracted."

"A dispensation for a softer time. Revelation showed us the error in this."

"Revelation," snorted my father.

"You can avoid your duty as a father no longer. You have refused this request too many times," said Thyenn Sharr. "This is not good for your son's soul."

"His soul? I will not offer him up to this year's Festival or any other. It is a useless affair."

"Useless?" shrieked Sharr. "It is a sin to refuse my direct request in this matter."

"Sometimes we have to suffer a lesser sin so that a greater sin doesn't overwhelm us. Violence against another is a sin too, Most Reverend, and yet the church condones it against the most helpless of us. It is wrong."

"Surely you don't mean that we shouldn't have the festival?"

"Have as many festivals as you like," said my father. "But this one? Where we Shame the Cursed? That has to go."

Sharr scowled at my father in a blatant display of disrespect. "It is a sacred ritual."

"It is racist, embarrassing, and does not honor the Unspoken who gave us these children."

"They are licentious sinners."

My father's hand came down on the table. "They are people, Sharr. Just like us. They cannot help their biology."

Sharr's face flushed with red blotches. "They incite men to sin!"

"I will not have you dishonor my deceased mate with such backward views in my own house. My mate did not incite me to sin. And I will not have you Shame my son, especially in the witness of the new ambassador. You heard him, Sharr. We need to get in their good graces, and everything I've read about them tells me they do not countenance racism, sexism, or bigotry."

Sharr stood suddenly. "You are a sinner, Aulkus Klath, and your child is a sinner born of sinners. You will not countenance me? I do not countenance you. Offer yourself for penance at the church, or you will regret your actions this day."

With a swish of his robes, Thyenn Sharr pushed past me without so much as a by-your-leave. Sharr's rude and imperious behavior caused a shiver of fear to run through my body even though I could not expect any other behavior from him.

When he was gone, I turned to my father. "What have you done?"

"I refused to offer you up for Shaming at Festival," he said. "And I will not repent for that."

Chapter Five

KAJ

Marta moved on the bed and turned on the light.

"What," I said with my arm thrown over my eyes.

"You're leaving me."

"What?" It was too late in the night for this conversation.

"I saw his eyes, that boy, with the golden, crystal shards in his eyes."

"You had a dream."

"Yes."

I groaned. "It was just a dream. Go back to sleep."

"It was real. Felt real."

"Marta, darling. I love you. Only you."

"You say that now. You won't then."

"And I told you. I won't accept any posting where we'd be apart."

"It won't matter," she said.

"Oh, for heaven's sake, why not?"

"I'll be dead."

I woke with a start, confused where I was. The damned heat surrounded me like an unshakeable shroud. There was no escape from it. I sucked in the sweltering air with each inevitable breath, and it was inside me and without. Sweat stained my clothes and the coverlet beneath. The dream shook me, gripping my heart with sadness. Even in one of our contentious moments I loved being with her. Missing her still hollowed my gut.

Was that why I took this posting, the farthest we've gone searching out our descendants? Was I trying to run from the pain of losing the only person I loved more than life itself? It seemed I couldn't go far enough, because she haunted my dreams.

I wanted those dreams, and they didn't last long enough.

A knock at the door brought clarity to why I woke where I slept. I had drunk too much wine and made an utter fool of myself. Arlan escorted me here, and I made an idiot of myself again.

Arlan.

The young man with the gold crystal shards in his eyes.

I had no faith in fortune tellers, or prognosticators, or reading auguries, but Marta described Arlan utterly. And how could she know him when he was half a galaxy away, and we had not found Ostakis then? Meeting Arlan was a weird coincidence or a cruel joke by the Universe, which had already played the cruelest joke of all—giving me someone to love at the end of my life.

"Ambassador?" It was the elder Klath.

I sat and rubbed my eyes. My head pounded, and I wished for the analgesic in my suitcases, which hopefully had been delivered to my new home in the city, wherever that may be.

"Yes," I answered.

"May I come in?"

How polite these people were. I may have insulted all of his guests at this man's table, but he spoke to me in total reverence.

"Please do."

Klath poked his head into the room and then entered. "I must offer my apologies."

"Why? I am the one who cannot hold my liquor."

"Oh that. Not a problem, Ambassador. But some of my guests were incalculably rude to you. My house apologizes to yours."

"Well, let's call it even," I said. "Because I dimly remember being a little rude myself."

Klath chuckled. "There is no rudeness in honesty. And my guests got a lesson in their place in the Universe. I think it was a good one even if it did not go down as well as my wine."

I tried to stand. "You are a magnanimous host." I swayed, and he reached to steady me.

"I think I should get you home."

Must I? I liked Klath and felt welcome in his house. But it wouldn't do. I was not supposed to show partiality.

"Will Arlan come with us?"

"Arlan?" He pursed his lips. "No. He's at work now."

"I like him," I blurted out. "He's a bright young man."

Aulkus Klath's eyes crinkled the merest amount. "You are aware he is contracted to a partner?"

"I remember that part of the conversation. I'm sorry if I caused offense."

"No. You didn't. Arlan resisted the contract for a long time. It is a partnership of convenience. I wanted something different for him." Aulkus pulled his lips into a solid line and then slapped his thighs. "Well, I imagine that you'll see Arlan from time to time. I expect that you will come to my house for dinner often, yes?"

"I would like that."

We traveled in an electric cart to a more modern part of the city, to a section that had a distinctly governmental look. Funny how humans do this regardless of where they are. The seat of government has a formal air and with broad and straight places, large enough to see from where your enemies come.

We turned down a street with expansive, sculptured lawns, and beds of exotic flowers and high, majestic houses. The driver turned into the driveway of one mansion. *This place cannot be mine*, I thought. *It is much too stately for a simple man like me.*

"This is it?" I asked, looking at the three-story monstrosity.

"I told them you needed a bigger house," he muttered.

"No. If anything, it is too big. You do not know how small the living quarters are on Earth."

He smiled. "Thirteen billion people on a planet smaller than this, only twenty-nine percent dry land? I suppose space is at a premium."

"I wish you could see Earth. The contrasts are quite amazing."

"But you have pictures, don't you? One night we will get together, and you can show them to me?"

"It honors my house you wish to do so."

"Come, meet the staff. Very agreeable people."

Of course, they would be. Most were government agents and would curry favor for information. I expected no less.

We walked a paved path edged on either side with willowy flowers whose petals looked like feathers. I stopped and marveled at them.

"These are not Earth stock," I said in awe. This was my first sight, other than holos, of plants of another world.

"No? We call them spiky stars. Irdrana insisted we plant them. We give them as a welcome, or to declare love. It shook her when she learned—let's just say Irdrana has always had a fascination with the homeworld. Your people's deaths devastated her."

Did he understand how much information he just revealed to me? "So you've known Irdrana long?"

He gave me an appraising glance as if trying to judge what to tell me. "It is natural we of the Upper House know each other. I've known Irdrana all her life."

I mulled Klath's reluctance to tell me more. These small tidbits about their habits and social structure spoke volumes. The Upper House must be tight-knit, perhaps interrelated.

A soft breeze blew in the humid air, but night was falling and the day cooled. A short portico framed an oversized front door, with carved panels showing men of different sizes cavorting in a garden.

What strange pictures for a society built on a conservative religion, I thought.

"You must forgive the history of this place. It was once a famous brothel."

Well, that shows what these people think of me. A government whore. "A brothel?" I asked incredulously.

"But the clerics have thoroughly cleansed it," he said solemnly.

"I'm sure."

He pounded on a square block inset in the center of the door. It ingeniously amplified the sound of the knock like a drum.

The door opened. A tall, thin man with a bald head and a close-cropped gray beard bowed.

"Welcome to the House Deder," he said.

"*Rasee Yinsi* Silar, this is your *yonsu*, Ambassador Kaj Deder."

"I welcome you to your house, honored *Yonsu* Ambassador Kaj Deder. Step over the threshold and claim this house as your own."

The threshold was a full straight piece of marble that could have been a step on its own. I stepped over it into my new home. For a second I panicked because my alcohol-sopped brain couldn't remember the ritual words. Then I caught them in the swirling soup of the language and my impressions of this planet.

"Let all know this house as House Deder and may it welcome all who come to it."

Silar nodded his approval, and I gathered this man was a stickler for details and protocols. Perhaps the Ostakian government thought I needed staff that adhered to rituals and rules. They couldn't be more wrong.

"Is there something I can get you, *Yonsu*?"

"The Ambassador has had a long journey and a stress-filled day," said Klath. "Perhaps he'd like a light night meal before going to bed."

"Excellent. Then I will show you to your room. Tomorrow we can tour the house."

"Yes. I would like that very much."

"In that case, I take my leave." He bowed. "Until the morrow, Ambassador. Irdrana Vos will come in the morning to bring you to your office."

"Your house has been more than gracious this day," I replied with a similar bow. Out of the corner of my eye, I noticed Silar studying each move I made and each word I spoke to see if I observed social forms. I planned to. To do so would build trust, and I wanted this man to trust me.

Aulkus Klath smiled warmly, bowed, and left me to the tender mercies of the stranger charged with my care.

The entrance to this house, like Klath's, had a high domed atrium painted a medium blue speckled with gold five-pointed stars, except for one with a flare and a cross of light.

"Do you like it?" asked Silar. "The committee changed the original design. That is Sol, your sun, shining on you from the distant stars."

The gesture oddly touched me. A few people cared about my welcome here. "And who was this committee?"

"I believe you have met them this day."

Ah, Klath, Vos, Sharr, and Seyatt. Prestigious people all, except maybe for Vos, that lovely woman. How did she get to such a high position? Or was the diplomatic mission here not considered of enough consequence to have a man head it? Was diplomacy considered woman's work? I put that idea aside as something to discuss with Klath.

"Have you changed the house?" I asked casually, not betraying my suspicions that they installed listening devices.

"No, *Yonsu*. There was the ritual cleaning, a long and tedious affair."

Ah, not a fan of the Faith Progressive Church. "I've received no materials about the church, Silar. Do such things exist?"

"Yes, *Yonsu*. In copious amounts."

"Can you get some for me?"

"I will endeavor to do so, *Yonsu*."

"You understand, it is more to learn about the people here. The church is an important part of their lives."

The barest tightening of the *rasee yinsi's* jaw, and how without question he accepted the pronoun "their" told me volumes about his dislike of the church. Silar nodded and pointed down a corridor. "Your room is this way."

"Did my luggage arrive?"

"Yes, *Yonsu.* I was in the middle of unpacking it when you arrived." He looked over his shoulder. "I hope the unpacking meets with your approval, as I was uncertain if it would please you or not."

"*Rasee Yinsi,* I appreciate the time and effort you take in my care."

He nodded again. We walked past several white doors inlaid with gold. I did not know if it was gold leaf or just gold paint, but it gave the doors an elegant, even ostentatious appearance.

Silar stopped at the end of the hallway and opened the door to an enormous suite that rivaled the size of my apartments on Earth.

"*Yonsu,* the sitting room," said Silar. It was a windowless room with couches and upholstered chairs lining three of the walls. It seemed like a receiving area.

He opened another door which led to a larger room. A huge four poster bed on the right came perpendicular from the wall, another sitting area formed by a large couch and end chairs sat on the left. But in front of me was a wall of paneled glass that overlooked a magnificent garden. Outside on the patio was a dining table with several chairs.

"And here, *Yonsu* is your toilet area."

He opened a door on the left. I peeked my head inside to find a luxuriously appointed bath with a tub the size of a small pool. That said a lot about my status here, since it was a desert world and water was at a premium. A bowl set on an elaborate table appeared to be the sink while a hole in the floor seemed to be the toilet. Oh well, one cannot expect all the comforts of home millions of miles away from it.

"Thank you, *Rasee Yinsi.* I am most pleased."

Again, I used a ritual response. Again, Silar nodded his head.

A knock on the door satisfied my curiosity about listening devices. A young, dark-haired woman brought in a tray, and Silar motioned with her to take it to the patio. *So, I thought. Not only is every conversation in the house listened to, they make no bones in letting me know about it.*

This was only the second woman I had seen in my short time here, and I was fascinated. She wore the same clothing wraps sported by the others I had met, but it was a cloth of meager quality. The young woman pulled her dark hair into a functional rather than decorative bun. She bowed at Silar and me and left the room without a word.

"That is Tenesea, one of the kitchen staff. She will bring you your food."

I wondered if "bring you your food" was a euphemism for something else. On some diplomatic missions, eager governments assigned staff to keep ambassadors "happy." But as lovely as Tenesea was, I had no interest in her. She was no Marta.

Or no Arlan.

Chapter Six

ARLAN

I walk with shame upon the earth,
For I bear the sins of my fathers within my body.
There is no cry, plea or prayer I can make
To make me whole,
Or to heal the sins that brought me to this state.
I am a sinner begotten of sinners, and I despair.
Cleanse me, Lord, for I am unclean,
Come that I do from sin
Cleanse me, Lord, of the stains on my soul
I give myself to Thee.
Make my shame known to all my fellows
As an example of your righteous judgment.
All I can be now is an example of what others
Need turn from.
Shame me, Lord, for the good of all.
—Faith Progressive Church Bible; Psalm of the Cursed

I waited for my father to return from escorting Kaj Deder to his house in the dining room because I wanted to talk to him about Pib. The front door opened and our *rasee yinsi*, Edemar, greeted him.

"Bring me some of the winter red wine to my office."

"Yes, *Yonsu*."

Edemar's ample feet slapped the tiles, and I stood to follow my father into his office at the right-hand door off the atrium.

"Father," I said before he shut the door.

His head swiveled toward me. "Arlan?" He seemed surprised. I did not often enter the public part of the house. I usually spent my time in the family part or my office.

"Can I speak with you, Father?"

"Is this important? I have much to think over."

"It is. I want to speak to you about Pib."

He motioned tiredly for me to follow him into his office. It was a somber room, for formal business, but since my birth parent died, Father spent as little time as possible in the familial part of the residence. Too many memories, my father said.

He sat behind his desk and rubbed the bridge of his nose. "What about Pib?"

"Father, Pib is in trouble. His parents sold a marriage contract for him to a trader in Kiji Amst."

"Which trader?"

"He did not say and could lack that information. But he does know the trader has a wife."

My father squared his shoulders and huffed his displeasure. "That is unfortunate."

My stomach roiled with nerves as I steeled myself to make my appeal. What I said next could change the course of Pib's life. "Father, I saved nearly all the money I've earned and banked enough money to buy his partnership contract."

"Buy his partnership contract?" Confusion washed his face, and I didn't blame him. It was an unusual request. "Buy his partnership contract? Why would you do that?"

"He is my friend, Father, and I do not want him to be unhappy."

"And what do you propose to do with this partnership contract?"

"Hold it until he finds someone he would like."

"And until then?"

"He'll work in my office. I have taught him much of the work. He'll be very valuable to us."

"You seem to have thought of everything, but one. What of Ushos Phale?"

"What of him?"

"He contracted *your* partnership. What will he say if you bought out the partnership contract of another?"

"I care not."

"I see that. But your partner, Ushos, will own your holdings. And he'll be able to do what he likes to Pib, perhaps even put him in a brothel. Have you considered that?"

I had not. Ushos Phale had been so far from my thoughts recently that I hadn't consider the ramifications of what he might do.

"It is a lucky thing that he has not made the final payments on your marriage contract. But still, son, the clock ticks for you, does it not? How many more heats can you have without mating?"

"Not many," I said in a soft voice.

"I'm aware you love your friend like a brother, and I've done nothing to discourage that. But his fate is his own."

"How can you say that? You oppose every law written against the Cursed."

He winced because he hated that title. "It is one thing to speak against it. It is quite another to break it."

"I'm not asking you to break any laws."

"Oh no? Allowing my son to purchase a marriage contract?"

"Then you do it," I said. My eagerness to help Pib overrode my good sense.

My father groaned. I went too far. "I do not have the heart for that, son. Since your parent died, I have no taste for another mate. I think I am too old."

"You are not."

"Pib is a child to me, son. It wouldn't do, and it's unseemly."

I sighed, knowing he was right. "Please forgive me. I'm worried about him. Pib is massively unhappy."

Father pursed his lips and knitted his brows. "Here is what I'll do. I'll talk to Pib's parents about making a happier arrangement for him. I know of a few unmarried traders who might welcome a bright young man like Pib. Especially since you have illegally tutored him in managing accounts." It was more than I hoped for but less than I wanted.

"Would you?" I asked. For things like this, I loved my father. Few men would care so much for a Cursed son.

He nodded. "But I want you to do one thing for me."

"What is it, Father?"

"I'd like you to stay away from the Earth Ambassador."

"What? Why?"

"He shows an interest in you. You know Thyenn Sharr set conditions to allow the Earth Ambassador to establish his Embassy. One was we do not tell him about the Cursed. And should you spend more time with the Ambassador, I'm concerned his interest would blossom into active curiosity."

"Oh," I said. It made sense. Sharr, because of his religious convictions, wouldn't allow Earth to find out about our sins. He wanted to present us as the pure race he imagined us to be. I wasn't sure about that. How much could we hide from Earth?

Why did the thought of not seeing Kaj Deder fill me with disappointment? It seemed unfair, somehow, that I could not even cross paths with him. But if my father could help Pib, that would be worth it. Pib deserved my loyalty.

"Of course, Father. I'll do what you wish."

The day had dissolved into early evening, and I hadn't eaten much at the aborted daymeal. I made a path to the kitchen and found Ija supervising the cleanup by watching Sharr's nightly sermon on the holo. The miniature of the cleric gazed out at his electronically connected followers spouting holy condemnation as he railed about the sins of unbelievers.

"What's for the evening meal?"

"Leftovers," she said. "I made sandwiches from the meat. They are in the cold box."

"Thank you."

"Take one to Pib," she said as I pulled out the tray from the large commercial cold box. My father often entertained, so he remodeled the kitchen to resemble that of a restaurant's.

"He's still here?"

"Oh yes, he came out here looking for sweets."

"That's Pib."

"There are some tarts in the lower drawer. They didn't reach the daymeal table." She sounded unhappy, but Ija was more than a cook. She was an artist with food. It disappointed her when people didn't appreciate her efforts.

"Thanks, Ija."

"It's that Earth Ambassador, isn't it?" she asked with reproach.

I stopped as I loaded a butler tray with sandwiches and tarts. "What do you mean?"

"He brings trouble, doesn't he?"

"No, Ija. He brings opportunity. They have materials and technology we need."

"He's an unbeliever. Remember, Arlan: 'Beware the unbeliever for he walks in unseemly ways and does not know his sins.'"

It was useless to argue with Ija on religious matters. Father put up with Ija's religious devotion because she was otherwise a kind soul who coincidentally was the best chef in the city.

The back door opened and someone I did not expect to see this day entered. And Ija was not pleased. Ushos Phale had but two inches on me in height, with unremarkable black hair and blue eyes, and a body most generously described as compact. It was his arrogant manner that carried him through most days.

"*Yon* Phale, why are you not using the front door as a visitor should?" she snapped.

Ushos bowed. "My apologies, *Rasee Yansi* Ija. My only thought was to visit my partner."

"He's not your partner yet, you reprobate."

What did Ushos want? He was one of my father's assistants and saw him daily in the office. There was no need for him to show up unless he wanted something from me. And there was only one thing he wanted from me, and I wasn't prepared to give it to him. Not yet.

"How about a game of chess, Arlan?"

"I have a visitor."

"A visitor?" he asked with suspicion in his voice.

"Yes, Pib."

"Well, send him away."

"I will not, Ushos. You should go now."

"You really should start being nice to me, Arlan. We are going to be together for a long time."

"Yes, we are. So there is no need to rush spending time together now."

Ija turned her head away and laughed into her hand.

I was at the counter with the tray of food, and Ushos moved behind me, putting his hands on either side of me.

"You have a heat coming soon," he breathed in my ear. "Wouldn't it be nice if we sealed our partnership then?"

"Ushos," I said. "The next time you want to visit, send a message ahead of you, and I'll see what I can do."

Ushos stepped away. "Fine." He let the screen door slam as he left.

"Some men are ill winds," opined Ija.

Perhaps Ushos was. But I didn't have many choices. There were not many unchurched men in Kiji Ost who would take a Cursed as a partner even if such a Union offered the trademaster post as a sweetener to the deal.

"Blessings to you, Ija. See you in the morning."

After navigating the hallways with an overloaded tray, I found Pib, sitting at his desk. The lamp streamed yellow light onto the accounts book.

"Are you hungry?" I asked.

He looked up at me. "How do you do this? I've been staring at these numbers all afternoon, and they aren't adding up."

"You've worked hard enough for one day."

"But the work isn't finished."

"That's the beauty of numbers, Pib," I said. I set down the tray and reached over his shoulder to close the account book. "They always work the same and are always there the next day. Here, I've some sandwiches Ija made from the daymeal and some of her tarts too."

"I should go home."

I looked out the window to see the light fading fast and didn't want Pib walking home in the night-cloaked streets. They were not safe for the Cursed after dark.

"Stay tonight. I don't want to be alone."

"Why? Are you coming into heat?" He was as aware of my cycles as I was of his. Mine was due soon.

"No. I have things on my mind."

"My father—"

"He should know where you are. It is either here or your house. I'll send a message over tomorrow. It is too late now to contract a messenger service. They are all closed."

"That late? Where did the time go?"

"Where it always does," I said. "One step behind you as you try to make another forward." I placed the tray on the bed and motioned for Pib to join me.

Pib retrieved two bottles of my hidden stash of beer. Not that my father cared, but Ija was fierce when it came to inventory and supplies. If she knew I had the beverage in my room, she wouldn't allow me in the kitchen for a month.

Pib consumed his meal as if he was a starving man. Afterward, we played a game of chess. But night fell fast, so Pib borrowed one of my nightshirts and we crawled into bed. He put his arm around me and drew me close. I sighed. One of the few good things about my life was my friendship with this man.

"You have been very quiet this evening," he said.

"Yes."

"What is on your mind?"

"The Earth Ambassador."

"Why?"

"I like him."

"I'm sure diplomats learn to be agreeable people."

"No, it is more than that."

"What is it?"

"He asked me to call him by his first name."

Pib whistled in appreciation. "He's forward."

"I don't think he meant it in that manner. And you know Sharr has forbidden my father to talk about the Cursed. He doesn't know."

"What is he like?"

"He is taller than father, though leaner. His skin is as pale as the moon, and his eyes are ice blue. And he is smart and observant."

"So," said Pib with a mischievous grin, "you have it bad for him."

My cheeks flushed. "What? No!"

Pib crossed his arms smugly. "Hah! You do so."

I rubbed the back of my neck. "I just met him."

"So? Isn't that what happened when your father met your parent?"

I looked away. "That's different."

"How's it different?"

Pib's challenge made me scramble to find how my father and birthparent's mating was different from Pib's dramatic fantasy of me and the Ambassador.

"For one thing, my parent and my father met at a festival. And my parent came from this planet."

"So? Perhaps your father will think joining House Klath with the ambassador's house beneficial."

I rolled my eyes. "And maybe you should get romantic ideas out of your head. Go to sleep, Pib."

I turned away from him and laid my head on my arm, staring out my window to the white Ostakian moon that reminded me of the pale ambassador from another planet.

Chapter Seven

KAJ

Dearest Marta,

I met him today, the boy with the golden crystal shards in his eyes. And he is beautiful like you said he'd be. Only he's no boy, but a young man. And I don't know him well, but he seems bright, and he's quick to smile, at least at me. Unaccountably, I am quite taken by him.

But you knew I would be.

How I miss you.

I am in the woods. It is dark, and I hold a flashlight in my hand. I am on patrol though what I patrol and where I am eludes me. The underbrush rustles, and I move forward to investigate. A man lies on the forest floor, unconscious with blood seeping into his clothes.
Sweeping my flashlight through the dark undergrowth, I see people fleeing. They are afraid, but they have left this young man in my care...

I woke with a start from loud noises coming from the atrium. Just a dream, then. I sighed. The gravity of the planet pinned my exhausted body to the bed like lead weights. There was no escaping the heat, and my mind spun a kaleidoscope of images. The jumble of my arrival, the daymeal, meeting these people, the ever-present sense of danger collided to produce a dream that had everything and nothing to do with the day. The moon now rose high in the dark sky outside my window. I hadn't been asleep for more than a few hours.

A loud, stressed voice floated into my room. I rose from my bed, put on my beige-silk robe, and cautiously walked the hallway.

"But I must use your sanctuary room," said a young man. "This house is a refuge, is it not?" His eyes were wide and his movements jerky. His brown curls flew wildly unkempt around his drawn face.

"No longer. Not now. The Earth—"

"What is going on Silar?" I asked my *rasee yinsi*.

Immediately Silar dropped his hands and bowed in his fastidious ceremonial manner. "I'm sorry, Ambassador. This is nothing for you to worry about."

"But he's crossed my threshold, and that makes it my problem, doesn't it, Silar?"

"Sir," appealed Silar.

"Well, I am *yonsu* of this house, am I not?"

"Yes, sir," said Silar. But his cheek jerked in a nervous tick. There was something he hid from me.

"So tell me, what is the problem?"

"This young man has made a mistake."

"Please," said the youth. He pushed past Silar and slid prostrate on the marble floor. "I beg asylum. I cannot walk the streets like this."

Asylum? No. I could not grant asylum to a citizen of this planet. I was supposed to keep abreast of politics, not embroil myself in them.

"What is he talking about?"

"I will call the authorities," said Silar.

"No," screamed the young man. "My family has disowned me. I have no place to go."

I look to Silar, whose face turned nearly purple with anxiety.

"There are public facilities," said Silar. "Officers will take him there."

"No. Please, please, good sir, you must let me stay. I'll do anything, anything." He licked his lips and stared at me, his gaze traveling down my body and centered on my groin. Man or woman made no difference to me, but it would be wrong to take advantage of a young, sick man. And at that moment, he appeared very ill.

"Call the authorities," I said to Silar.

"No!" blubbered the man. He was beside himself and buried his face in his arms on the ground sobbing. I bent next to him and touched his shoulder. What should have been a moment of compassion turned into something else.

The next thing that happened was so amazing that I didn't believe what I heard or saw. The young man purred a cat-like sound and rubbed his face on my arm and then caught my hand as I pulled away. He rubbed his face on my hand and trilled louder. But my physical reaction caught me off guard. Immediately my cock grew harder than it had ever been and my one thought was to fuck this beautiful stranger into oblivion.

"Sir, sir," said Silar, pulling on my shoulders. "You must go back to your room."

The young man licked the palm of my hand, and I shivered. If it weren't for Silar yammering in my ear, I would have ripped his pants off and taken him in the middle of the atrium on the marble floor. Thoughts of decorum or comfort absented my mind.

But my brain, not my cock, recognized the sense of Silar's words. I was hardly a day into my mission and had screwed up enough for one day. I could not afford a scandal, and my job was not to fuck the indigenous population. Shakily I stood, and with great difficulty, steered myself back to my room and then locked the door.

The scent of the man clung to my hand. Drawn by a primal need, I sniffed it with my back against my door. My breathing quickened, and my heart thudded in my chest. My cock still stood stiff, unyielding and throbbing, and if I did not do something about it, I would go insane.

I gripped myself and stroked the length as I thought of the young man who wanted what I had to give him. Again I thought about ripping his pants from him and burying myself deep within him, pounding the young man senseless until I spilled my seed inside him. My mind exploded, and I erupted into my hand hot, sticky, copious amounts of come as if my body drew every single last bit of fluid from it.

When it was over, I sagged against the door, breathing hard, while I struggled to regain my reason. I had never come so hard from masturbating and felt thoroughly drained.

But the man's scent clung to me, and already my balls tingled, and I wanted to take myself in hand again. Hot, and exhausted from the events of the day, I sought my bath, and drew a lukewarm one hoping to cool my overheated and overwrought body.

The water was a welcome balm and eased the weight on my overworked muscles. But even as my body relaxed, my mind spun. Why did the man in the atrium act so strangely? From what was he seeking asylum? Why was he afraid to walk the streets in "his condition?" And what condition was that?

After a day of strangeness, the night was even weirder.

The next I knew a hand shook my shoulder, and I jolted awake. Groggily and stupidly I stared at the man.

"Sir," Silar said. "You mustn't sleep in the bath."

He was right, and I felt the fool.

"Would you get me a towel, please?"

"Yes, sir," said Silar neutrally. I stood as cold water shimmered down my body and the humidity of the planet hit me again. With his eyes discreetly turned to the side he held open the towel, which I wrapped around my body.

"Did the authorities take the young man?"

"Yes, sir. They will look after him now."

"I wonder why he came here?"

"I don't know, sir," Silar replied. He kept his eyes averted, and I perceived he was lying.

"He said something about this house being a refuge."

"The young man made a mistake."

I thought about the pictures of the men cavorting on the front panels of the door and that Klath said the house was once a brothel. But was it? Or something else?

"Did he seek refuge here another time?"

Silar closed his eyes and refused to answer.

"It will not work, me being here if you keep secrets from me," I said.

Silar's jaw set.

"I'm sorry, sir," said Silar. But he did not indicate why he was sorry. For keeping secrets? Or that I clumsily insulted him? I had no way of divining that as Silar's face remained stubbornly neutral.

"By your leave, I give you to the rest of the night," said the *rasee yinsi.*

"Thank you, Silar."

He left, every moment manifesting serene grace regardless of circumstance—the perfect servant.

Yet, even his title said he was no servant. *Rasee yinsi* translated as "housemaster." Or did I make a mistake in grammar and it meant master of the house? My title—*yonsu*—roughly translated as "lord," but even that wasn't right. By me occupying this house, this place became Rasee Deder, the House of Deder, and that name would display on electronic maps of the city. But the parameters of my new station eluded me. Silar managed the house, and the servants and their activities. He treated me more like an honored guest than as the person legally responsible for what transpired under my roof. Either there was some display of power that I failed to make to assert my authority, or I was a figurehead that in title held authority but in reality did not. Could *Rasee Deder* be just "the place where Kaj Deder lays his poor, foolish head while we who run things laugh at him behind his back?" It probably wasn't as dire as that, but maybe there was a shade of truth in that assessment.

I sat, then put my feet on my bed as the humidity rolled over me in waves. My body, exhausted from fighting the long day and the gravity, gave up its fight to stay awake. *Tomorrow though*, I thought before my eyes fluttered shut, *I'll find out what happened to that young man.*

Chapter Eight

ARLAN

The day started quietly enough. I ordered a messenger to deliver a note to Pib's family to inform them that he stayed with us last night. Father was gracious enough to sign it and even stamp it with his wax seal. I sent it ahead of Pib's arrival to his home while we breakfasted in the garden.

The gardens were almost as old as this house, which nurtured twenty generations of us Klath. Our gardener, Tolen, a Cursed like Pib and me, tended the lush beds of flowers. He was elderly, and there was never a time I did not know him. But Tolen bowed as Pib and I came to the ironwork table that sat under a stately feather tree. Its long fronds arched and bent toward the ground dancing in the day's light breeze.

"Tolen," I scolded. "You needn't bow."

He bowed again. "Begging your pardon, *Sid-Yonsu* Arlan."

I sighed. I wasn't a master anywhere, but Tolen insisted on giving me a master's due.

"The feather tree is looking lovely."

"Yes," said Tolen. "But cullen blight it." He offered his hand to reveal a cullen egg, wrapped in larval silk. I stared at it in alarm. Cullens were valuable for their silk, but their propagation strictly regulated because of their danger to vegetation.

"You will register this with the Ministry of Agriculture?"

"Yes, *Sid-Yonsu* Arlan. *Rasee Yansi* Ija is composing the letter and arranging the messenger to send this sample."

"Very good, Tolen. And you can save the tree?"

Tolen sighed. "I will endeavor to do so. But if I can't eradicate the infestation, then I must burn the tree."

What a sad thought. My ancestors planted the tree in the original garden. I held many memories of days the tree sheltered me in shade from the heat while I read and studied.

"I understand," I said. "The most important thing is that the infestation doesn't spread."

"That is why I am spending the day turning over everything. If it goes beyond the tree, we may have to destroy the garden, and I would hate that."

"We appreciate your dedication, Tolen. I am sure whatever you need to do is in the best interests of House Klath."

"Thank you, *Sid-Yonsu* Arlan." He bowed again and walked to the house leaving Pib and me alone.

A servant girl I had not seen before this day brought our breakfast of scones, tea, and fruit. She did not bow as she set the tray on the table but merely stood with her hands folded.

"I have not met you," I said.

"I am Senesea."

"And is this your first posting?"

She shot me a look that expressed I did not have the right to ask her that.

"No, *Syad* Arlan," she said. So no "master" title for me. The new housemaid correctly identified me as the son of the lord of this house and as a Cursed. No. She would not elevate me above her station. She may be a maid, but I was the lowest of the low.

"I see you Walk in His Glorious Name," I said, barely keeping the sarcasm from my voice. Church connections may have bought her this posting, which meant I should take care around her.

"We all bear the stain of sin," she said piously.

"Walk in joy," I replied, dismissing her.

She nodded and left us to our meal.

Pib whistled. "Wow, she acts as if she came straight from the House of the Faithful."

"She just may, Pib. Thyenn Sharr would like nothing better to have one of his Holy Nuns spying on my father for him."

"No. Not even Sharr could be that reckless."

"You think not?" I opened my mouth and closed it. I almost told Pib about the events of last night when my father and Thyenn Sharr argued. But I shouldn't gossip about a discussion I had no right to hear.

"Say, I talked to my father about you last night."

His face colored as he took a sip of his tea. "And I suppose he will bargain for my partnership contract," he said. The sarcastic edge in his voice fluttered like a leaf in the wind.

"You were quite correct that he wouldn't intervene in that way. But he said he would talk to some traders in the town who might have an interest in making a partnership with you."

"Really?" Pib's face brightened with a smile. "If anyone would—" He stopped as his face colored a brighter red. "I'm sorry. I didn't mean to imply—"

"What? That my father knew all the sinners in town?"

"On hell, Arlan," he said, staring at his scone.

"Stop it, Pib. My father feels no shame in lying with a Cursed man. He and my parent shared a loving relationship."

"But—"

I folded my arms and stared at him. "But what?"

He swallowed hard. "Your father was married."

"Yes. That was before his partnership with my parent. What of it?"

"It's confusing. The church says a man who knows the cleansing love of a woman isn't incited to sin."

"What?" And then I got it. Pib's proposed partner was married and yet wanted a Cursed as a lover. He paid good money to do so.

"I mean how did your father decide—"

"You'd have to talk to him about that," I said, knowing Pib never would. The church annulment between my father and his wife was a tremendous scandal that few rarely talked about these days. "All I know is that when my birthparent and my father met, that was it. Father contracted the partnership and came to live here."

"Despite Most Reverend Sharr," said Pib.

"I think Father would say in spite of Most Reverend Sharr. And Pib, it scares you. Hell, it frightens all of us Cursed. When our heats take over the men or we have no choice. And knowing there is only one result, a child, makes it scarier."

"I do not know if I can stand bearing a child for nine months," he said. "My mother constantly complained before my younger sister was born."

"Your mother is melodramatic."

"But many of us Cursed die in childbirth."

I sucked in a breath, and Pib gazed at me, shocked at the depth of his social stumble. My birthparent, Segun, died in childbirth with his second pregnancy. It was after that my father decided he would raise me with as many freedoms as he could grant.

"Because the doctors don't want to attend our births," I said with disgust. "It is a crime, or should be, how they treat us."

Pib gnawed his lip. "I don't want to die."

I put my arm around him and drew him closer though it was clumsy to do so between our two chairs.

"Why," he keened, "did the Unspoken curse us with their blood?"

I rocked him, trying to comfort not just him but myself. "My father says they didn't have much choice. They were a simple people, tribal, and the first colonists exploited them in all ways."

"Sharr says the Unspoken incited the colonists to sin."

"Do you believe that? Have you not witnessed enough sin among our people to know the hardness in men's hearts? If the colonists were that cold in their regard to an indigenous people, then they deserved the Unspoken's curse."

"Sharr would beat you for that heresy."

"He would beat me anyway," I said bitterly.

"I do not want to die in childbirth," said Pib.

"You won't," I said with simple faith. The Lord of All could not take Pib Alluven away from me.

"And I do not want to go to Kiji Amst," he declared.

"I agree. I do not want you so far away from me. Who else will I beat in chess?"

Pib laughed.

The hinges to the gate at the side of the house creaked, and I looked up to see my father enter. Beside him was Pib's father wearing a deep scowl. My father pointed to us at the table.

"See," he said. "Just as I said."

Harth Alluven was a man whose belly had seen too many beers and his chin sported a thick gray beard. His skin was very dark, mostly from his enthusiasm for golf and the many hours on the links. I never saw the appeal myself. When he is entertaining, he is as jovial as Pib. But now his face wore the rage of a wronged man.

"How dare you stay out all night," he spat. He strode toward Pib and raised his hand. Pib shrank close to the garden wall.

"Now, Alluven," said my father. "The young man is fine. It is not that he hasn't spent the night before."

"That was before his promised partnership. How do I assure his partner that nothing unseemly happened here?"

Father's face furrowed, and anger flickered in his eyes. "Because I give my word of honor such," he rumbled.

It took a lot to get my father angry, but Harth Alluven had pushed him to the edge. My father guarded his reputation for honor fiercely, and all in Kiji Ost knew it. But Harth hated that he produced a Cursed son and saw Pib as evidence of the sin of his forbearers, just as Thyenn Sharr preached from the pulpit.

Alluven stared at my father but then looked away. His next move was to grab Pib by his underwrap and pull him forward.

"Harth," growled my father. "Pib is a guest in my house. Take your hands off him."

"He's my son." Harth Alluven glared at my father a shade long enough to display his displeasure but not to draw an honor challenge.

"No longer. You sold him to the highest bidder." My father stared back but he did not care how long he did. A man who challenged Aulkus Klath took his life into his hands.

"How dare—" snapped Alluven.

"Do not make me call a challenge, Alluven. You cannot prevail over me."

The color drained from Harth Alluven's face because all knew Aulkus Klath's reputation. He never lost a challenge. With Alluven's courage failed he turned to the one person he could bully. "Pib, come with me now."

"Pib, stay where you stand." My father placed his body between the two Alluvens. Did he mean to brew a challenge? It would be a convenient way to rid Pib of the obligation to the Kiji Amst trader.

"You overstep, Klath," growled Harth.

My father scoffed. "Why are you concerned? You don't want him anyway."

"How I handle my family is my concern, not yours," said Harth indignantly.

"So, now he's family? Not a commodity to sell on the open market?" Father held his ground and didn't allow Harth to move forward.

"What? Your son is in a contract?"

"That is different. Arlan made his own choice."

Alluven moved forward ready to push my father away, but thankfully my father stepped away suddenly causing Alluven to stumble. My father chucked and Alluven shot him a look that could kill.

"Pib," ordered Alluven. "Come with me now."

"You're disgusting," said my father. He spit on the ground. "Selling your son to a trader who has a wife."

"I'm doing nothing illegal. And for the good of his soul, he should partner."

"And his children are of no consequence?"

Alluven stared at the ground.

"Your grandchildren, clanless. Without a house. There is a difference between illegal and immoral, Alluven. Spare us from the laws if they cause a moral harm."

"Like you know the difference, Klath. You parade your Cursed son around as someone to be proud of, appalling all of Kiji Ost with your cheek. Thyenn Sharr will strip you of your arrogance."

"Why? Because you are not man enough to do it yourself?"

Alluven sputtered incoherently, and that tempted me to ask my father if he wanted his sword. But Father didn't let this argument go that far. No. What he did next shocked us all.

"You are so interested in selling your child? Here."

Father pulled a roll of currency out of his pocket and threw it to the ground at Alluven's feet. The Building Master's mouth opened because a small fortune lay there, probably ten times what he got for Pib from the trader. Alluven could buy back the contract from the merchant and give himself a handsome profit.

"Take it," rumbled my father. "And be grateful that I do not report you to the Civil Courts for abusing a person charged to your protection."

Pib's father hissed in the manner of the Unspoken. It was a hollow sound full of warning and menace, and signaled Alluven was about to lose control. It was gauche and socially unacceptable to make those sounds.

"You will not get away with this, Klath. I will bring you up on charges for holding my son against my will."

"Do it," said my father. "You come into my house and abuse my hospitality by attacking my son's guest. Then you insult my honor. And then refuse an excellent deal for your Cursed to a family that will provide for him better than you ever could. So go. Do your worst. I'll remind you of one thing, however. I can afford better lawyers than you."

"Curse you, Klath and your child. Pib, either you get home within the hour, or your friends will pay for your insolence."

Alluven strode by my father and slammed the garden gate shut.

My father bent and retrieved the roll of money.

"Well," he muttered, "at least Thyenn Sharr won't complain I didn't pay the tithe money on time."

"Father," I said as my throat thickening with gratitude overwhelmed me. I was at a loss as to how to thank him.

"I think I should go," said Pib. His face drained of color, and he stood shaking.

"No," said my father. "I've had enough of these abuses. Go to the sanctuary room and stay there. If authorities arrive, I will say that you are in heat and will stay with us until it is over."

"Trademaster," said Pib, "I do appreciate your concern for my welfare, but I cannot allow you to face the consequences of my father's wrath."

I had a terrible feeling I wouldn't see Pib again if he left this garden. "Please, Pib. For my sake, do not leave."

"It is for your sake I do, dear Arlan. Do not worry. He'll only beat me a little. He wouldn't want to damage the merchandise."

Chapter Nine

KAJ

"I do not want you to go," I said.

She kissed my cheek. "It is for my dissertation. I have to do this to finish school."

"No, you don't. Not there," I said. "Not in a place ready to blow apart at the slightest ill wind. Go someplace else."

"Let's not fight," she said. All we'd been doing is fighting since she lost the baby.

"I'm not trying to fight you."

"Good."

"I just want you to be safe."

"Sweetheart, we did not go into the Diplomatic Service for safety. Please kiss me. I have to go. Robert will be here to pick me up."

"Robert," I said sourly. "So you are going with him."

She shook her head with a rueful smile playing on her lips. "It's for school. I'll be back, I promise."

The scene turns, and I'm in the Rathskeller with my buddy, Charles. We were playing darts when I got a text.

It was just such a poor way to do this. I sat hard in my chair. I may have lost her before she left, but I did not expect this.

"What's wrong?" said Charles.

"Marta," I said.

"What about Marta?"

"She's not coming home."

Every muscle and bone ached when I woke, and I succumbed to the standard issue painkillers allotted for this mission. I must use them sparingly. Their use was to help me over the hump of adjusting to the increased gravity of Ostakis, and they did not give me many. But they were moderately strong, so, no wine at lunch for me.

As if that was a good idea.

Silar knocked and entered.

"*Yonsu*, would you like to view the house?"

"Do I have time?"

"Yes, Ambassador. You have a few minutes before Ambassador Vos arrives."

How seamlessly Silar moved from "*yonsu*" to "ambassador." I would have to remember that words are specific to functions and not interchangeable as they are on Earth.

I had so much to learn.

Silar moved me through the immense, elegant house. A towering staircase of darkly polished wood wound in a graceful arc to the second floor. He waited patiently for me as I took the stairs as if I were an old man. At the top of the staircase, I stopped and sucked air in stutters.

"Are you ill, Ambassador?"

"No. The gravity on this planet is heavier than my—" I had to stop saying "my planet." Since taking this job, I could no longer claim that planet as home. I could never return to Earth.

Silar waited as I caught my breath. I held up my hand to stave off his attentions. "Heavier than Earth. It will take me a while to adjust."

"Oh," he said. "I was not aware. Forgive me, but may I ask a question?"

"Of course."

"Is your health in danger while adjusting to a world with heavier gravity?"

I stared at him. It was an extraordinary question, and I did not expect it.

"I only ask, *Yonsu*, because it is part of my duties to see to your health and in this, I appear unprepared."

Yonsu, again. At once I was touched and appalled. Responsible for my health?

We did not discuss that much, those of us who went through the Diplomatic Service curriculum. In fact, there was only one class for one hour where we touched on it. The reason the HPC paid the recruiting bonus to our families was the enormous risk First Posting Ambassadors faced when we stepped on a different world.

All the reasons a person faced death on Earth tripled when they walked onto another planet. Radiation, infection, murderous intent, political scapegoating—the risks were countless. And the further we travelled from Earth, the odds of death increased. That was why they send only one of us at a time. We, the first legates, are expendable.

But how could I tell this to my *ransee yinsi*? I couldn't.

There were reasons. First, there was the issue of trust. How could I establish that if I said I expected to die within the first year I live here? Second, I did not want him to think that I regarded my life lightly. I did not.

"I appreciate your service, *Ransee Yinsi*. The Diplomatic Core doctors assure me that I am in perfect health. The process of acclimation, while uncomfortable, will finish in a few months."

He bowed, saying nothing, but I saw the wheels turning in his mind.

"Forgive me. Perhaps, *Yonsu*, we shall walk more slowly for today? So you can acclimate without stressing your heart too much?"

Oh hell. Silar was taking this much too seriously. How should I answer that? "I thank you for your concern."

He showed me the rooms, bedrooms, filled with luxurious furniture and whose walls were different colors. I could see my mother, a regal woman, saying, "Silar, take our guest to the green room." Mom would love this place.

He showed me all the rooms except for one. At the end of the hall was one door, and if my sense of direction served me correctly, was directly above my room.

"What is that room?"

Silar's face formed a pinched expression. "Storage," he said.

Again, I sensed he was lying. But Silar took his duties seriously, so there was something in that room he thought would jeopardize my mission, which made me want to see it all the more.

A loud noise of rapping on the front door rang through the house.

"Excuse me, *Yonsu*. I must answer that."

"Go ahead. I'll take my time, so as not to stress my heart."

Silar nodded and rushed off.

I put my hand on the handle. My heart beat hard as I turned and opened the door.

It was dark, and as I touched the walls to search for a light switch, my hands brushed thick padding adhered to the walls. I found the switch and the light illuminated a featureless room. The same dark padding covered the walls, the floor, and the ceiling.

What the hell was this place? Why did they have a padded cell on the floor of the guest bedrooms? Did they expect to imprison me here? Were they afraid I would go mad and have this prepared just in case? Many wild thoughts crossed my mind, and none of them made sense.

This room creeped me out.

I shut the door and backed away, wondering what this room meant.

"*Yonsu.*"

I jumped, for I was so immersed in my thoughts I did not hear the *ransee yinsi* climb the stairs.

"Forgive me, Yonsu. Ambassador Irdrana Vos is waiting in the atrium for you."

"Thank you, Silar. Please tell her I will be with her presently."

"Very good, *Yonsu.*

I took my time walking downstairs. For the second time within as many days, I fought gravity as I descended the mammoth staircase. My heart thudded in my chest as I eased one foot after another down the steps. If I fell, my nonacclimated bones would shatter. I had never felt fragile before. It was a new experience.

Irdrana smiled as I entered the atrium. "Good day and health to you, Ambassador Deder."

"And to you also, Ambassador Vos."

Silar opened the door for us, and once again the indomitable Ostakian heat assailed me. Irdrana wrapped her arm around mine as we walked to the cart.

"The Trademaster told me you planted the spikey stars to welcome me," I said.

Irdrana uttered a small sound of dismay. "The man can keep nothing to himself. But, of course, I desired to show you Ostakis welcomed you, Ambassador, despite the impolite words of others."

"You mean Thyenn Sharr."

"Now, Ambassador, you know the Most High Reverend only intends to sow the Holy Word for the good of our souls."

"I love how you do that," I said.

"What?"

"Speak inoffensively when you mean to give offense."

"It is a talent," she said. She gave me a sly smile.

Irdrana settled next to me in the electric cart, and we made small talk as the driver took the transport through the elegant streets of this section of Kiji Ost.

Our conversation, however, stalled and then Irdrana looked up at me with earnest eyes. "Forgive me, Ambassador, but I must ask."

"Yes?"

"You are young, are you not? For this position?"

I nodded and hid my nervousness. What should I tell Irdrana? That there may come the point where my youth and fitness will be more important than my experience at the job? I did not want to dissemble, but I was hoping I could accomplish my mission without implementing the final solution.

"The expanded HPC mission to find former colony planets has taxed the diplomatic service's supply of personnel. They now issue higher education scholarships for those who commit to serve."

This was true enough. What I did not add was this did not apply to me. As the son of an ambassador, his benefits paid for my education. But I saw I must move this conversation along.

"Ambassador," I said. "On Earth, a large city will have names for different sections. Is this true in Kiji Ost?"

"Why, yes, Ambassador," she said with a bright smile. "We call this one the Garden District. Aulkus Klath lives in Dastoan Heights, and our destination is Church Point."

"Church Point?"

"You'll see."

And I did. The Garden District gave way to the modern buildings of downtown Kiji Ostak, but the cart turned north instead of south away from the spaceport. I caught glimpses of the sun dancing off the water at the end of the streets.

"That is Lake Veller," she said.

"Veller? As in the captain of the colony ship?"

"Very good, Ambassador."

"Please, call me Kaj."

She smiled brightly again. "Kaj. And please call me Irdrana."

"I am pleased to do so."

"Thank you, Kaj. I know I will find it pleasant to work with you. In fact, I already do."

We passed by the most massive construction I'd seen on this planet to date, what could only be a church. Spires reached high in the sky, and the rock-faced building sunk behind shadows created by large columned porticos that framed it.

"Yes," Irdrana said as she watched my mouth gape. "The Faith Progressive Church."

"It is—huge." It was the most polite thing I could say. The edifice itself was ugly and out of place in this section of the city.

"Yes. Lakeside space is at a premium, and we can use every bit for trade with other cities, but the church refuses to move."

"Why would it move?" I asked. The idea that a church would move was an extraordinary one to me.

"When we founded Kiji Ostak, we clustered around the lake for obvious reasons. The predecessor of the Faith Progressive Church received a grant of land just as all other colony entities did. But as we grew, the city council embraced city planning. Those different businesses and entities that had nothing to do with trade exchanged their grants for others in the newly established parts of the town. The Faith Progressive Church refused, saying it needed the water from Lake Veller for Cleansings."

"Cleansings? Is that a religious ritual?"

"Yes." She sighed. "The traffic from supplicants clog the roadways. This annoys the Trademaster and others, especially during religious festivals, which are all too frequent."

"You don't sound like a fan of the Faith Progressive Church."

"Among professionals, like myself, the Church has little appeal. It speaks to the masses who accept its precepts without question."

"Interesting," I said. "And yet Thyenn Sharr was on my welcoming committee."

"Most Reverend Thyenn Sharr has money and influence. He was the one who donated your house as your residence."

"He did?"

Irdrana laughed as if remembering a joke. "A penitent left it to the church in his will."

Now I understood her mirth. "Trademaster Klath told me it was a whorehouse."

Irdrana stopped laughing. "Oh, my. I guess I shouldn't be laughing."

"I'm not offended. At least I know where I stand with Most Reverend Thyenn Sharr. And it is a lovely house."

"It is. And most houses don't have such luxurious tubs."

"And it explains the overabundance of bedrooms."

Now she laughed heartily.

"People assured me, *twice*, that Sharr's people thoroughly cleansed the house."

Irdrana now doubled over in giggles.

"You do have a sense of humor, don't you Kaj?"

"Some have accused me of that from time to time."

"I wish you could have been there when they did it. Fifty novices dressed in dark robes walked through the house with incense and doused the walls with holy water. It was quite the scene. And poor Silar was beside himself worried they'd stain the silk furniture with the water."

"How did you stay straight-faced?"

"Oh, I couldn't. I had to pretend to cry for the sinners into Trademaster Klath's shoulder. He was quite gracious about it."

"Silar called it a tedious affair."

"Oh yes, it went on for *hours*."

Irdrana, in the implacable throes of her mirth, clutched her stomach.

"Ambassador Vos," said the driver in a disapproving voice. "We approach the Trade House."

Irdrana did her best to pull herself together. "I'm sorry," she said and let loose a string of giggles.

"No apology needed. I was beginning to think no one laughed here."

The cart stopped at the door of a five-story brownstone building. People streamed in and out as a testament to the economic power of this place.

"Come," she said. I followed her inside. It reminded me of the buildings of Old New York until I got inside. Intricate mosaic patterns decorated the walls and floors.

"I love this building," said Irdrana. "It doesn't seek to deny who we are."

But before I could ask her what she meant, a man rushed up to her and bowed. "Ambassadors—Trademaster Klath asks to see you right away."

"Thank you," Irdrana said. Her face drew into a solemn mask, and she waved for me to follow as she entered an elevator. I clutched the handrails as the ascent added to the heaviness I felt. After leaving the car, we walked down a long hallway lined with chairs, all empty. She did not knock when she entered the door.

"Uncle," she said with urgency. Klath looked up from his desk and then down again, writing on a document. His hand moved furiously, and then he appeared to sign it. He put the pen in its holder and sighed and looked up.

"Irdrana, witness this," he said. He pushed the paper to her, and she looked at it with alarm.

"Uncle?"

"I heard Sharr will send his Holy Guard to arrest me. I have to safeguard my work, and my home."

She glanced at me in alarm then back to Klath.

"Have you discussed this with—?"

"I don't have the time. This is my will. Sign it, Irdrana. I do not know when they will arrive."

She put her signature on the draft, and he pulled a lighter from his pocket and heated a small wax candle. He dripped two pools of wax, and Irdrana pressed the top of her ring in one. Klath did the same with a ring on his hand with the other.

"It's done," he said. He pulled the ring from his finger and handed it to me.

"Take this."

"What?"

Raps on the door drew Klath's and Irdrana's attention.

"She will explain it to you. With luck, I'll be home this evening. If not, walk with the Lord, Ambassador. Seyatt is a friend, and Irdrana will help you all she can."

The door burst open, and even I could recognize the look of military men.

"Aulkus Klath," said one. "You are under arrest by order of the Faith Progressive Church, and you will hand over your ring and seals of authority."

"You can arrest me," said Klath, "but I've assigned my authority to another."

"Who?"

"Ambassador Kaj Deder."

The soldier who spoke pursed his lips as tightly as if he'd eaten a lemon. "Let me see the writ."

Irdrana held it up but did not let the man touch it. "It is legal. I witnessed it myself."

"But he's not from this planet."

"He owns a house and has gainful employment. That's all that's needed."

A guard put manacles on Klath's wrists roughly, but Klath grinned as if he pulled a fast one on Sharr. Which, I suppose he did.

"Take care of Arlan," he said over his shoulder as the guards pushed him through the door. His eyes pleaded with me while I stood speechless at the sudden turn of events.

Chapter Ten

ARLAN

I tried to concentrate on the account books, but I was restless. Thoughts of Pib worked my mind. I disliked that he blithely walked off for his father to beat him "only a little." He could have stayed, and my father would have protected him. Father was wary of breaking laws, but he despised how our society treated the Cursed. Was Pib hurt? Did they lock him in his room? These thoughts occupied my mind instead of my work, and there was nothing I could do. As heavy of heart as it made me, Pib chose his fate.

The work Pib finished the day before spread before me, and even I had a problem spotting the mistake that caused the error in the numbers. I examined the previous month's work and found no errors. I pulled the receipts and the deposit slips and on a separate sheet of paper redid through the calculations.

The problem wasn't Pib's calculations. One deposit slip transposed the numbers. My father would have to speak with the client about the error so that *yonsu* could fix his bank account.

With a sigh, I went to the kitchen to see if there was food, but it was not time for daymeal yet. I picked a leftover tart from the cold box, but after one bite decided I didn't want it. I walked to the garden and strolled the walkways wishing Pib walked with me. Suddenly I did not want to be alone, and even the thought of spending time with Ushos Phale appealed to me.

And then it hit me.

My heat was upon me.

Why did this always surprise me? It happened twice a year, though this one seemed to be closer than the last. Hells. I never enjoyed spending a week in the sanctuary room howling my head off.

I walked to my office and wrote notes to my clients telling them I had to shut the accounting office for a week. There was nothing for it. Then I entered my father's office and lined up the message cylinders marked with the color and names of the houses. Father would sign, seal, and send them off.

My hands shook while I worked signaling the severity of my oncoming heat. I had waited too long to mate, and my body would punish me for it.

Edemar entered my father's office. "*Sid Yonsu?*"

I trilled involuntarily, which was never a good sign. His face registered alarm.

"Perhaps, you should go to the sanctuary room," he said, his face losing color.

But a rap at the front door drew his attention. "Wait here."

I stood staring at my hands as if they were of great interest. With a heat's start, the shifting hormones affected brain function. Soon I would be nothing more than a mass of sexual need. But a great commotion at the door snapped me to attention.

And a particular scent.

Not of this world, but utterly masculine.

Mine.

In all my heats since puberty, I had never had that thought. There was never one man that I would want to call my own.

Until now.

My heart raced in my chest, and my palms sweated.

Irdrana Vos brought a stunned Kaj Deder into my father's office, took one look at me and threw her arms around him protectively.

As if I would attack him.

But it was an appealing thought.

She muttered under her breath.

"What's wrong?" asked Kaj.

"Edemar!" snapped Irdrana. "Arlan is not well. Get him to his room."

"Yes, Ambassador."

"What? What's wrong?" repeated Kaj.

Kaj. My Kaj. Sweet Kaj. I reached out to him as Edemar escorted me with both hands on my shoulders out of the office.

My body warred with my head as I fought to go with Edemar to the safest place in the house for me and all near me.

I trilled again to call him, my mate.

"Listen," said Edemar urgently in my ear. "Sharr arrested your father. Your father handed the authority of his office and his house to Kaj Deder, so the church cannot confiscate it. Do you understand, Arlan? Kaj Deder is the *yonsu* of House Klath now."

"Good," I said, not comprehending the gravity of anything but that *he* was in my house.

Edemar sighed with exasperation and walked me to the door of the sanctuary room then opened it. "I will check on you later."

Edemar shut the door on me, just as he should, and comforting darkness surrounded me. A lack of light helped, but I suspected not today. I was much too edgy.

And he was here.

I wanted him.

I sunk to the corner of the room, taking comfort in the sensation of the padded floor touching my body. That would not last long. Soon my hormones would kick into mating mode, and I would cry and keen for a mate.

Only there was only one mate I wanted now.

Though the room's construction did not allow for scents to pass in or out, I caught it anyway. I brought my hands to my nose, and his musk was there.

I had touched him.

Kaj.

A trill escaped my lips, expressing my longing for him. And the trills did not stop weaving an ancient song, one older than before humans stepped on this world.

Where was he? Why did he not answer my call?

My clothes scratched my oversensitive skin. I tore them off in a flurry of activity and threw them in another corner of the room. Then I sat with my arms around my knees and rocked.

And trilled.

This was different, oh so different from other heats. My mind focused on a single individual, and all my yearning and need centered on him. My body burned with desire.

The man with the crystal blue eyes.

Kaj!

Minutes or hours made no difference. I needed him, now, with me. Only he could calm the fire that raged in my body and my mind.

The cramps hit me striking with actual pain. My heart beat wildly, and I clutched my arms across my stomach as I rode the wave of one agony after another.

My trills now became demanding yowls.

Come to me.

I repeated those words over and over as if they were an arcane spell that would draw my lover to me. Tears came to my eyes because of the pain and because I needed him so very much.

Now the pain and the tears wracked my body in concert.

The door creaked open, and a shard of light peeked through.

"*Yonsu,*" said Edemar. "You shouldn't—"

"Nor should you lock up Arlan. I do not understand this. Get out of my way, *Ransee Yinsee.*" His voice was strong and commanding.

I loved his voice.

"Arlan?" he asked.

"Here," I said in a small voice.

"I cannot see him," Kaj said, sounding thoroughly annoyed. "Where is the light switch?"

The bright light of the single overhead bulb burst upon me. I covered my eyes.

"Arlan? Are you okay?" Kaj asked.

He walked toward me. Edemar shut the door, but he did it quietly. The *ransee yinsee* knew just as I did what would happen. There was no stopping it now.

"They incite men to sin."

Kaj knelt next to me. "What's wrong, Arlan?" he asked.

"Nothing," I said. The last thing I wanted was talk right now.

"How can you say 'nothing'? Are you upset about your father?"

What was wrong with my father? Something sat in the back of my mind, but all I could think about now was Kaj, how he knelt next to me. My nostrils flared open, taking in his male scent.

The black of his eyes widened, and Kaj shivered as he touched my face. I shuddered at the pleasure of his flesh against mine. I grabbed his hand and purred into it, rubbing my cheek against it, trilling in my delight to press his flesh against mine.

"Arlan?" His voice trembled.

I lunged. He backed away, but I moved faster. We fell to the soft floor, made that way for this very reason. I covered his body, and my lips crushed his mouth, hungry for his taste and velvet flesh. I sought his tongue, and our mouths danced against each other, lips and tongue, and heat and need. It all tumbled where we were no longer two separate people and fire lit my body.

I did not know it would be heaven.

He rolled me onto my back. He looked at me with half-lidded eyes as he rained kisses on my neck and behind my ear. My back arched and I yowled. I needed so much more than this.

Kaj continued his assault sucking on my neck, my nipples, my abs, and then my shaft.

Oh, good God above, my shaft. My back arched again and my toes curled, but it was a sweet torture because I could not come like this, not in my heat.

"Please," I keened.

I knew what I wanted, what my body needed. I was frustrated, and I yowled again.

"Damn," he said after he pulled off me. His strong arms flipped me again. "On your knees."

I loved the sound of command in his voice, but I was weak, boneless, so he jerked me up with a growl, and pushed my knees under me.

"Yes," I said.

Something soft was at my hole, teasing it with flesh, and with a shock, I realize it is his tongue.

"Why do you taste so sweet?" he growled again.

I keened a long, high note. I could wait no more, and I pushed my ass into his face.

"Now," I said between gritted teeth.

He pulled away, and I was at a loss. What was happening? But I heard sounds, and it got through my lust sodden brain that he was removing his clothes. Each beat of my heart was but one word.

Wait.

Wait.

Wait.

Waiting was the worst. I wanted Kaj *now*.

My need was all instinct. I had no idea what it would feel like when I got what my body demanded. I had never taken a heat to completion.

Flesh pressed at my hole. I was ready. I wanted this. But it was not what I expected. I looked over my shoulder and saw he pushed his finger inside me.

What was with all the preliminaries?

I yowled, seeming the only vocalization I could make.

"You are wet?" he asked in astonishment.

I keen again and push my ass into his hand.

"I get it," he said. He pulled his finger from me, and I could feel his body tremble. He wanted this as much as me.

"Fuck," he said as he pushed the head of his shaft into my hole. His hands gripped my hips as he slid into me.

It was glorious. Him gliding against my walls as he filled me, overwhelmed me. I gasped.

"I haven't hurt you?"

It was a strange question. *Hell no*, I wanted to say. But I could barely speak.

"More," I groaned.

Slowly he drew back and pushed in again, but I hung on the edge of completion. The fire in my body raged, and it needed a partner who could keep up with it.

Chapter Eleven

KAJ

Dearest Marta,

You believed I did not forgive you for losing our child. I think about this often and wished I could have done better by you. You do not know how much guilt I feel in this.

Yes. I wish you did not take that assignment in an area of the world in so much turmoil. That you did not flee into that job to escape the bitterness of what happened. I wish I were there the day that suicide bomber stepped into the hall in which you spoke. I wish—

There are so many wishes, but my most fervent is you knew I never blamed you, that I could have told you that before I lost you forever.

What the fuck was I doing?

I was inside Arlan, out of control, and my body shook with the absolute need to fuck him. My efforts to slow things down, to get a handle on this utterly failed.

I wanted to fail.

Arlan pushed against me and made that noise again, one that was utterly entrancing.

He wanted me.

He needed me.

Good Lord, I needed him too. I couldn't stop this if I wanted to, and I didn't.

I took his hips in both hands and rattled us both with my rutting. My violent need overtook my mind, and soon my balls slapped against his with the push and pull of our rhythm. My heart was a runaway train and my breathing chugged, but I pounded into him, taking everything I wanted and needed. The pull of the muscles in my stomach and rush in my balls told me I careened toward the inevitable. But I was not selfish, and I reached around and jacked his cock with my hand.

He groaned, and he tossed his head, and it was the most entrancing thing I've ever seen. The muscle on his neck that ran to his shoulder bunched prettily and suddenly, despite everything that was going on, I needed that flesh in my mouth. I clamped down on it, teeth and all, with a primal wildness that surged through my soul, and he screamed. I loved the sound. The walls of his body contracted around my cock in spasms, and he came in my hand. There was no holding off now. I clutched his hips as I slammed hard into him, and the world flew off its axis, and stars danced behind my eyelids. Fire burst through me, white and hot, and I shot my seed deep inside him. I kept pouring into him with ragged thrusts into his willing body until there was no more of me left and my balls were empty.

He shuddered under me as I collapsed on his back. I rolled us both to the side, and I clung to him, kissing his neck, telling him how wondrous he was.

And he was. I loved my wife, but I suspected I would love this man more.

Arlan sighed. "You bit me," he said dreamily.

"I'm sorry," I said.

"Sorry?" he replied, and he sounded hurt. "You did not want to claim me?"

"Ssh, ssh." I stroked his hair. "Not that. I thought I might have hurt you."

"Why do you think that?"

"I sunk my teeth into your skin?"

"It will heal quickly," he said.

"You were delicious," I replied, smiling into his shoulder.

"Good, because I want to taste good to you. Irresistible."

"You are."

"As you are to me. See?"

He turned to face me and pressed his hardened cock into my thigh.

"I need a few minutes," I said.

"Do you?" he said, glancing down at my cock. It was filling again and want and need shook me once more.

"Make love to me, Kaj," he said.

And we did, countless times, until I was a hollow shell of a man.

Exhausted, I fell asleep. I woke to the aroma of food. Arlan scarfed it heartily, sitting naked and cross-legged, from a tray laden with fruit, cheeses, and meats.

"Grab some while you can," he said. "I've never been so hungry."

"I can't imagine why," I said, pushing myself to sit.

He pushed me back down. "No. Don't get up. Rest and eat now. You'll need your energy."

The way he said it, in all seriousness, made me wonder what was up other than Arlan's voracious appetite.

"Why, Arlan?"

"Well, my heat isn't over yet. Here, try the mollusks. They help speed a man's recovery."

"Arlan?" Impossible questions formed in my mind. "What do you mean 'heat?'"

He cocked his head and bit his lip. Then he sighed. "They did not—would not tell you. It's complicated, and I suppose we'll have a long talk about this, but my kind carry the reproductive parts of both genders. Outwardly, we look like men, but inwardly—"

I held up my hand. "Stop. But you aren't a woman."

"That's right. I'm a Cursed."

"Cursed?"

"It's what they call my kind. And if you are wondering why the entry point is what it is, it's supposed to be. Made for that. Serves a dual purpose. The entry spot of a woman—well, in us that opens only for the birth and then seals again between children."

I furrowed my brow. "Birth? Children?"

"That's the point of a heat," he said matter-of-factly while munching on a piece of fruit. I swallowed hard as I watched Arlan's mouth, entranced as he ate the slice, and unbidden, an image of his mouth on my cock captured me. I shook my head to clear it. Why was it so difficult to concentrate? Arlan's musk permeated the air in this closed space and my shaft twitched. Good lord, I couldn't imagine I had the strength to make love to him again. And yet my cock hardened.

"You mean, you expect to get pregnant from-from what we did?"

"If we are lucky, yes. The first time doesn't always take."

I got to my feet and paced. What did I get my ambassadorial ass into?

"Kaj? What is wrong?"

"Wrong? Wrong?" I raged. "What the fuck is this, Arlan? Are you telling me that what we did was all pheromones and reproduction?"

Arlan lowered his head. "You're upset."

"Damn right I am." My thoughts jumbled in confused disorder, and I couldn't make sense of what Arlan said. No one lied to me overtly, yet my heart ached with the sting of betrayal. Not that I didn't want Arlan. I had from the first minute I saw him. I had control of that. But when I walked into this place, I had no restraint, not a single iota. If I had known, would I have entered this room locked against the world?

The color drained from Arlan's face and hurt shown in his glorious eyes with the golden shards, and I felt like the biggest ass in the world.

"Then you wouldn't want my child," he said. Arlan's voice sounded as if I cut his heart as it beat in his chest.

Instantly I fell to my knees before him and took his hands into mine.

"Arlan, I'm sorry."

"That's okay," he said as tears formed in his eyes. "I understand. I incited you to sin and put my burden on you."

"What? No!"

"No. I understand. There are drugs I can take after. You needn't worry about the burden of a child."

I sat in stunned silence gazing at this man who blew up my world. This was too much to contemplate. I'd wanted a child for so long but never thought I'd have one with a man I found hundreds of light years from my home. How could I?

"You must get them, of course," he said matter-of-factly. "I'm not allowed to purchase them on my own and Father would never keep them in the house."

"Arlan?"

"You should eat," he said pragmatically. "You will need your strength."

"Arlan," I said more forcibly. "No child is a burden."

He lowered his head. "And if I do not want a child from a man who does not want me?"

"Oh for heaven's sake!" I exploded, and Arlan flinched and pushed away from me.

"Arlan, I'm sorry," I said again.

"You are my *yonsu*. I will do what you say.

I put my hand over my mouth, agog at the number of cultural conventions I stumbled over in the past two minutes. What concepts! He was to blame for my lapse of judgment? That he is to take the consequences of creating a child? Or bear a child he might not want? What madness was this?

"Arlan, please be patient with me. I've no experience with this."

"You've gotten no one pregnant?"

"That's not what I mean. What I mean is when I have sex with a man, I don't expect to get *him* pregnant."

"Have you had sex with many men?"

"That is none of your business," I said too harshly. His face fell. "At least not yet. Give me a chance to get to know you."

"You want to?" he asked, his face more hopeful.

"Yes, I do, Arlan. But should we create a child, it will be your choice if you keep it or not, and I will support whatever decision you make."

"You will?"

"Yes."

"And you'll stay with me as my mate?"

"Let's not get ahead of ourselves."

"Oh," he said, his face falling again. "But you are right. I still have that partnership agreement with Ushos Phale. He wants me if only to gain the Trademaster post."

"What?" I was outraged. I did not know who this Ushos Phale was but if he so much as touched Arlan, I would rip his arms off. And while that piece of information about the Trademaster post surprised me, the thought of someone wanting Arlan for his inheritance angered me.

The ferocity of my reaction took me aback.

I took his hands again and instinctively licked the juices of the fruit he had eaten from them. Arlan smelled of fruit and sex, and I remembered the delicious musk of his entrance. It was an exotic thing that he should be slicked and ready for me there. It was not what I was used to. But I liked it.

He shivered at the touch of my tongue on his palm and closed his eyes. I pulled away because I was surprised at my reaction so soon after my completion. But I was ready, and I wanted him again. How far did I want to take this? Could I get up and walk away? My mind tried to imagine it. A soft kiss on his cheek, comforting words and—

My mind could not go there. I could not leave Arlan. Not yet. And it overwhelmed me too. When had that ever happened? Once. With Marta, but only then. But Marta was not here and would never grace my life again.

Arlan was here, sweet Arlan with his willing body and a need that rivaled my own. Still, I was in a delicate situation. Aulkus Klath was in trouble, and he made me his agent, transferred the care of his business, House, and Arlan. Where did I stand? What actions could I take, or should I intervene at all?

Arlan took my hand and trilled into it while eyeing my excitement.

"Arlan. I cannot make promises. There is a lot to consider. You, your father, my job, the political situation. It is too much for any man on any one day. I need time to think, and that is not happening now."

"This is not the time for promises, Kaj. We have now. The rest will wait until we've finished. We will sort out the world then."

"Are you sure?" I asked.

"If you wish," he whispered.

"I do," I replied. "Do you know what else I wish for?"

"What?"

"That you lay on your back and open your legs."

Chapter Twelve

ARLAN

I woke sated and relaxed. Gone was the edginess that drove me insane. The haze in my head slowly cleared. I should savor this moment of relaxation. But words spoken yesterday buzzed formlessly in my head, trying to find a place to arrange themselves into coherence.

All that mattered right now was Kaj. He lay next to me, his lanky body sprawled out, arms and legs spread wide. I had seen nothing more beautiful. I could glance at him now without the buzzing in my brain that drove me to act like an animal when I lay near him.

I stared at his strange clothes tossed into a corner of the room. Kaj's garments fitted his body like a sheath and came in parts. His footwear was like that too, unlike the sandals we wore. I touched the boots and sniffed his footwear. I liked that scent, strong and masculine and somehow trustworthy? Yes. This man, a near stranger, was worthy of trust. But my father believed it, too.

The cold realization that my heat finished in one day hit me. I was not used to this. I'd spent up to seven days making a ravening fool by my unsated body before it gave up its quest to get me pregnant.

So now it was time to go back to the real world.

That's what I hated about my heats. The world stopped as my body focused on its overriding biological imperative.

The whole house could burn down around me, and I wouldn't care. Not until the heat was over.

House. Why was Kaj at the house? What had Edemar said to me? The horror creeped on me as I remembered his words.

"Sharr has arrested your father. Your father handed the authority of his office and his house to Kaj Deder so the church won't confiscate it. Do you understand, Arlan? Kaj Deder is the yonsu of House Klath now."

Sharr arrested my father. I felt sick that my heat robbed me of reason and my father sat in a jail cell at the Faith Progressive Church. I found my clothes in the corner of the room and dressed. There would be time for clean-up later, but I must discover my father's status.

Kaj stirred. "Arlan?"

"Thyenn Sharr arrested my father."

Kaj sat up quickly and gazed at me with concern. "Yes."

"And he gave you legal authority over House Klath."

"Yes. Though I don't understand what all that means."

"Get dressed. There are things we need to do."

"God, yes." He scrubbed his face with his hands. "Good lord, I don't know what came over me. Arlan, I'm sorry."

I looked at this man from another world, and I apprehended there was much he did not understand. So I knelt before him and took his hands.

"Kaj. You have nothing for which to apologize. You are a stranger to this world, and in only one day, you've fallen head first into a situation that few can navigate. There are things they kept from you because Sharr is a man who hides his prejudices within his morals. And I'm sorry for the whole planet, because we do not deserve you and you do not deserve this treatment. Please, get dressed. We need to get my father out of jail, and right now you are the only one who can do that."

He did what I asked with questions in his eyes, while I worked to get Edemar's or Ija's attention. Finally, the door creaked open as Kaj pulled on that strange footwear of his.

Ija stared at us with wide eyes. Not that she didn't know what happened. I'm sure her husband, Edemar, told her. But it surprised her that my face had lost its heat flush, my pupils were not as wide as the moon, and I was relatively calm.

"Irdrana Vos is here in your office, *Yonsu*," she said to Kaj.

He sighed, then squared his shoulders. "You coming?" he said to me.

"As you wish, *Yonsu*."

He shook his head as if he didn't believe his new position. I didn't blame him. What my father did was unexpected.

I led the way as we walked to my father's office in silence, but he reached out for my hand and stopped walking. We were in the main hallway of the family part of the house. No one else was near.

"Arlan?"

"Yes?"

"This was crazy your father did this."

"Not if you know my father. He believes you are an honest man, and that counts in a big way to him."

"I don't see how he could trust me, when I, I..." He stopped, at a loss for words. "Arlan, I'm not the type of person to take advantage of someone."

"Why are you saying this?"

"I took advantage of you."

"Please," I said. "You didn't exactly have a choice."

"I don't understand."

"We have to talk about this. But later. Right now, we need to get my father out of jail."

He nodded, and my heart went out to him, especially when we walked into the office together, and my cousin stared at Kaj with her famous dagger stare.

"You've been unavailable for an entire day," she said coldly.

I gave her an imploring look. "Cousin, it wasn't his fault."

She scoffed. "Don't give me that. He's not from here. He shouldn't—"

"Irdrana," said Kaj evenly. "I'm right here."

"He's every bit a man as those from this planet, Irdrana, so I thank you for not lecturing him," I said.

"Arlan, I can fight my own battles," he said.

I bit my lip to keep my mouth shut.

"But," said Kaj, "we need to get Aulkus Klath released. How do we do that?"

"A solicitor files a petition to show cause for 'detention of arrested persons.' The court needs to respond within a day to explain the charges and reason for confinement."

"And does Aulkus have a solicitor?"

"Of course. He's in the Church Point District."

"Then we should go."

"The way you both look? I don't think so. I'll go and have him hammer out the papers. Just write me a note specifying me as your agent in this case. I'll also have him file the papers that name you as the yonsu of House Klath. I have the paper Aulkus signed. In the future, make sure that you hold onto any papers of that nature. Often there is only one copy, and you need to be able to produce it."

"Then write it out, Irdrana and I'll sign it. My written Ostakian is not proficient."

Irdrana wrote the note while Kaj and I stood behind her. Kaj looked at me, and I nodded. The letter said what it should, but I would expect it did. I trusted Irdrana just as my father did. That was why he pushed for her to have the official ambassador post. This was another thing my father did that Sharr hated. The Most Reverend wanted the position for one of his sons, but my father and Mar Seyatt were afraid he'd twist the ambassador post for the Church's benefit.

The Church needed no more benefits.

Irdrana demonstrated how to use the seal of office, and Kaj took my father's, now his, ring out of his pocket and pressed it into the dripped wax. When he finished, he attempted to put the ring in his pocket again, but I shook my head and took the ring and found a finger on which it fit. His hands were larger than my father's, so instead of the index finger, it fit on the one next to the little finger. Kaj blushed then, and I didn't understand why.

"I haven't worn a ring here for a long time," he said.

"You need to wear it," I said. "It shows your authority."

"But it isn't my authority," he protested.

"It is," said Irdrana, "because the one who held authority before you gave it to you. And until you give it to him or someone else, it is yours."

"Then I'll give it to Arlan."

I shook my head. "No. That would be illegal."

"Why?"

"Because those of my kind aren't allowed to hold property or public office."

His mouth gaped in shock. "That's crazy."

Irdrana pushed back her chair. "Learn more about us before you make that judgment. Go, get ready for court. I'll send a car for you to bring you to the Church."

I reached out my arms and kissed my cousin on the cheek.

"Thank you, Irdrana."

She touched the bite mark on my neck lightly and whispered, "Are you happy with him, Arlan?"

What could I say? She made assumptions about my relationship with Kaj now that we mated, but he made no pledges, and I agreed. He did not know what he was getting into, and I could not hold him to any promise because of that.

"He is all I could ask for," I said.

She patted my shoulder. "Good."

I took Kaj to the bath in my room after I asked one of the housemaids to find some of my father's clothes for Kaj. He eased into the tub as I ran the water, then he asked me to join him. It was a tight fit, but I liked it. I sat on his lap and he soaped my body. Kaj wrapped his hand around me to reach my front.

It felt good. Intimate in a way I never shared with anyone else, and I sighed, especially when his desire pressed against my bottom cheeks. Perhaps my heat wasn't quite over, or I just wanted him, but we enjoyed each other in that bath. He murmured sweet words in my ear, and I allowed it because I did not know if we would have this time again.

I helped him dress, winding the strips of gauzy undergarments around his legs, torso, and arms.

"Oh," he said. "I wondered about that. I thought it was a single shirt and pants sewn together."

"No. We used to do this to help keep the sand from our skin. Now it is just custom."

Kaj laughed. "I am the mummy," he said in his own language in a low and menacing voice.

We'd been speaking Ostakian, but I helped my father practice while he was learning Earthspeak, so I understood a few words but not the last.

I cocked my head. "What?"

"Nothing. Just a reference to an old myth."

"You will have to tell me about this myth."

"We have many."

"Even better," I said, without adding that I hoped he'd stick around to tell me all of them.

I wrapped the overgarment around him, gathering it in my hands quickly from long practice and draped it low on his hips, so it fell at his knees. Because he was so tall, I had to stand on a chair to get the top portion draped properly over his right shoulder. And his height precluded a flourish knot at the top. Such a knot was appropriate for his new station, but impossible because of his height. I used one of my simple brooches with the Klath insignia to hold the gathers at the shoulder. Then I tucked the rest of the drape in the waist of the wrap.

I clasped the brooch around the gathers. "This belonged to my parent."

"Aulkus?"

"No, my birth parent, Sigun."

"Oh," he said, and Kaj blushed again.

"It is only a loan," I added hastily. He nodded. "Only because it is a family heirloom. The House Klath has a long line of birth parents to it."

"Oh?" A confused expression etched on his handsome face.

"The property of this house descends through children such as myself."

"But you said you couldn't own property."

"That's right. Our fathers or mates legally own the property, but Cursed children of the union inherit. The law is part of the original charter of this city drafted before the Faith Progressive Church formed."

"Are you telling me that this Ushos Phale you talked about would get all of your property?"

"Yes. Including the Trademaster post when my father died."

"And this would be the House Phale?"

"No. The name goes with it. That is why when we present you at the court you will be Kaj Klath."

"Oh." His face scrunched in distress, but I couldn't help that he was uncomfortable with all of this.

The underwrap was a bright blue and the overwrap brown. These two colors highlighted Kaj's skin color and eyes. I raked my gaze over his body.

As I put sandals on his feet, I gazed up at him. "You are very handsome."

"And you," he said, staring at my nakedness, "look delicious."

"That may be so," I replied pragmatically, "but we now need to help my father."

Chapter Thirteen

KAJ

I was thoroughly shocked. So much had happened in the space of two Ostakian days, my mind couldn't keep up.

I stood in Arlan's room as he dressed me in Ostakian clothes. He worked precisely, so what he put on me was art instead of just protection for my body.

The gauze wrap was surprisingly light and let my skin breathe. I saw where this was much more appropriate for the heat here instead of my cotton button-down and khakis. He used separate strips on each leg. Then he palmed one end of a new roll and made a loose square knot on the top of my thigh and wrapped my hips. Arlan brought the strip above my shaft. He wound it over my hip, around my waist and crossed down the other and under my leg. My beautiful lover turned it and brought it up and around again, this time covering my shaft. He did this several times to secrete my phallus, leaving my balls to hang loose. I had to admit that I appreciated the freedom there. My anus likewise had no covering directly. All I had to do to use the bathroom was pull apart the gauze in front. No muss, no fuss.

Practical people, these Ostakians.

He wrapped my torso and arms completed an attractive *V* pattern up my chest and arms. He wound the overwrap on me quickly, his hands moving too fast to follow. When he finished, I wore a cross between an Indian sari and a Roman toga.

As he slipped a pair of sandals on my feet, he told me I looked handsome. But all I could think was that this intelligent, beautiful man was much more than I deserved. I wanted him again, but he told me, most practically, that we had things to do.

Arlan was right, but that didn't make me stop wanting him.

A warmth spread in my heart, and I smiled at Arlan like I was a schoolboy. He frowned as he dressed. And why shouldn't he? I told him I could make no promises, and I can't. But here I stood with a goofy smile as I gazed at my lover. I must have confused the hell out of him. He was in good company. I was befuddled too.

I marveled at the speed of his hands, and the flexibility of his joints as his brown skin disappeared under a dark red underwrap and then a blue overwrap. He was beautiful in the grace of his body and the determination on his face.

What I had learned was Arlan had no legal rights. He could not hold property or legally make decisions for himself. He lived at the mercy of his *yonsu*.

I could not imagine this. It was foreign and entirely overwhelming that it was my responsibility to not just care for this property but take care of this young man who may carry my child.

It was also beyond me at the moment to figure how all this would play out in my diplomatic mission. I did not make a favorable impression on Thyenn Sharr on my arrival. Now that I held a position he wanted for himself? Surely I was on his enemies' list.

Arlan answered a knock on his door. "Thank you. We'll be right out."

He looked at me. "The car is here. We should go." Gone were the smiles and sensual glances that preceded this moment. The world shifted once again and plunged me deeply into Ostakian politics. But before we went out that door, before the wider world intruded on what Arlan and I shared, I pulled him into my arms and kissed him. He melted into it, and the kiss turned tender. But that was all it was. We had business to attend to, and Arlan reminded me of that by pulling abruptly away from our embrace.

He led me out of the house, and we climbed onto the electric cart that passed for transportation. The heat hit me again, and my bones complained about moving in it and the thick gravity. A wave of exhaustion strikes me, and if I could, I'd go back to sleep. But Arlan needed me, and I owed him my help.

"Faith Progressive Church," said Arlan. The driver glanced at me for confirmation, and I got angry for Arlan. Why should he suffer such an indignity? Why was he not considered reliable enough to even give an address?

"Yes," I said.

"Very good, sir," said the driver.

Arlan stared forward with a determination, and his dark eyes glittered with sharp intent. He appeared as if he was riding into battle.

"Arlan?"

"Yes, *Yonsu.*"

"Call me Kaj."

"I will, *Yonsu*, in private."

I sighed. This world was too foreign to me. I did not understand it. Or rather I did parse it, but it repulsed me. Earth learned long ago that it is senseless and wrong to devalue any person. We no longer have religion, not in the sense that these people do. Instead, the general population subscribed to a set of principles. One is, "All prejudices are lies."

I saw the force of how much the Ostakians lie to themselves. People clogged the streets in dark gray robes, bumping in to each other and muttering. Even I, here only two days to this planet, knew them to be part of a great group bent on bad intent. Happy people did not press against each other in a throng to reach a destination. Joyful people danced and sang.

There was no dancing or singing here.

Black was the color of nothingness, but gray was the color of sin, a stain on the soul. But I gathered that sin here differed greatly from the concept I grew up with. On Earth, the greatest wrong is treating another person as less than yourself.

"Arlan, tell me. What is the purpose of Shaming?"

He frowned. "Truthfully? I've always thought it is to make people feel better about what they are instead of what they are not."

I took his hand between our bodies. Arlan spoke his words with a seriousness that belied his apparent years. Young men shouldn't have to be this serious, but then maybe that was one trait we shared.

"Yes, but what does the Church say about it?"

"The Cursed bear the sins of our fathers in our bodies. Shaming the Cursed shows a penitent's commitment to rejecting sin and living a godly life."

"And how does this Shaming occur?"

Arlan closed his eyes as if remembering horror. "They chain the Cursed to the Shaming post. Sometimes they strip him naked. Then the penitents shout insults, sometimes they throw things. They whip the Cursed if he has committed a legal crime. If it is an especially onerous crime, they whip him to death."

I squeezed his hand tighter as my stomach threatened to revolt. "Why would a *yonsu* allow this to happen to one under his care?" I did not understand this, could not.

"The Holy Texts say submitting to Shaming is a great benefit as it purifies the soul of the Cursed. A Cursed that submits to Shaming can enter Heaven upon their physical death." Arlan's voice was bitter, and I did not blame him.

"And ones that do not?"

"Languish in hell."

Heaven. Hell. All concepts that Earth discarded long ago. We still talked about them in philosophy classes and had a good laugh at the ancient concept of sin. One student among us would observe that hell seemed preferable because the sins that condemned you there were far more pleasurable than the graces that put you in heaven.

But hell here was far more palatable and more frightening. Hell was being born into the wrong body and living with the consequences as if it was a choice.

Arlan's hand was between us and I squeezed it. Arlan kept a reserved manner in public, but his distress ran through me as if it were my own.

I did not know what to say.

The electric car jolted on the cobbles of the road and the driver constantly blew the horn to clear people from our path. Individuals would throw dark glances our way as if we blocked their progress toward heaven. Arlan gripped my arm tightly when a few of the throng shouted things in Ostakian I did not understand.

"What are they saying, Arlan?" I asked.

"They call us sinners."

The angry invectives seemed to have more weight to it than what he said, but aside from holding my arm, Arlan's face was more determined than ever.

"We have a proverb from one of our ancient texts," I said.

"What is that, *Yonsu?*"

"Let he who is without sin cast the first stone."

"Excuse me?"

"Sorry. An ancient punishment was throwing stones at an individual to kill them. One great teacher stopped a stoning by getting in the middle and speaking those words. Then he wrote in the sand a sin committed by each one about to throw stones until the crowd dispersed."

"He sounds like a great man."

"He was. Some thought he was God."

"I think," said Arlan very seriously, "that all men hold God within and in some God shines more brightly than others."

"That sounds about right."

The crowd pressed around us, and the driver stopped to avoid running people over. For the first time, I spotted law enforcement. They dressed in black and carried thick sticks.

"Who are those, Arlan?"

"They are Church Police. The Church tasks them to keep order on Festival Days."

"Is there a civil police force?"

"Yes, but they do not perform crowd control. They investigate crimes and make recommendations on whether the matter goes to civil or church court."

A civil or a church court. This was something not in the information packet. Truly the First Contact team had glaring omissions in their work. But then, they didn't get a chance to complete it.

I noticed I have not seen a single child here and I wondered at that.

"Arlan, why do I not see children at this festival?"

"Children are innocent until they experience the first cravings of the flesh. They do not need redemption, yet." Arlan's grip on my hand tightened. Ahead I spotted the dark spires of the Faith Progressive Church. The car halted with a jolt that threw us both forward.

"Forgive me, *Yonsu*. I cannot go farther," the driver said.

It was a miracle he got this far. The driver handed me a clipboard. "Press the ring into this area."

"I have no wax," I said.

"Unnecessary," Arlan said. "The paper is a kind that will darken at the pressure point."

I did the deed and handed back the clipboard.

"Thank you, *Yonsu*. May fortune find your house and dwell within."

"And your house as well."

Immediately as we descended from the cart, two Church police appeared out of the throng. Arlan's jaw set and his expression communicated his discomfort at this turn of events.

"Ambassador," said one. "Most Reverend Sharr sends us to facilitate your arrival."

How did Sharr know we would be here? Arlan's expression was angry but not surprised. I gave a small flourish of my hand and pointed to the beastly edifice that dominated the landscape showing my assent. One blew a whistle, and the other held out his hands on either side forcing an opening in the thick crowd.

Like Moses parting the Red Sea.

Scholars wrote no miracle parted the sea because the water they passed over was a reed sea. The Jews made their way across it by wading through the shallow water. The chariots of the Egyptians floundered in the reed clogged byway, and the Jews made their escape. But the Bible recorded the parting of the waters story, which was no doubt crafted to highlight the powers of the new God at the cusp of the Age of Aries.

And perhaps the only reason it came to mind was that the Age of Aries signaled the rise of the age of war and patriarchy throughout the earth. In that battle of the ages, the goddesses lost and were relegated to the background. How strange that must have been then.

How strange it felt now. I was not used to this, where because I was male, every word I spoke was authoritative. That my signature and not Arlan's completed transactions. That I, a stranger to this world, had more power than the man who walked next to me.

It was too much. My cognitive dissonance was on overdrive and despite my training on melting into other cultures, my brain fought this furiously.

We grew close to the steps and Irdrana Vos stood on them surrounded by penitents, but she was recognizable because she was dressed in bright-colored clothes. She was a beacon of reason and sanity in a world where there appeared to be none.

Chapter Fourteen

ARLAN

The dark spires of the Faith Progressive Church rose against the cityscape as we turned the corner. I was glad Kaj sat next to me even though he looked away and his face displayed he was deep in thought. The trip to the church took twice as long as it should because penitents clogged the streets for Festival. I shivered because this Festival, The Shaming of the Cursed, was the one most feared by all of my kind.

There were frightening tales of Cursed ripped from their beds at the midnight hour and chained, half naked, to the Shaming Post. Ostensibly these Cursed had committed crimes. But the crimes could be as small as talking back to their *yonsu*. Or taking a crust of bread from the kitchen without permission, or just for the crime of existing. The Shaming could be light or horrific depending on what deals the Cursed's family cut with the Faith Progressive church. A sizable contribution to the Church bought lighter punishments. Redemption was not without its price.

"Arlan, tell me. What is the purpose of Shaming?"

I frowned. Like many Cursed, I tried not to dwell on it. It was the sword at the throat we lived with, always present as a background to our lives. But to contemplate its existence would drive a person mad.

"Truthfully? I've always thought it is to make people feel better about what they are instead of what they are not."

Kaj's hand covered mine, and I was grateful my strong *yonsu* was with me. Even if allowed, I did not know if I had the inner strength to face Thyenn Sharr alone in the heart of his domain.

"Yes, but what does the Church say about it?"

"The Cursed bear the sins of our fathers in our bodies. Shaming the Cursed demonstrates a penitent's commitment to rejecting sin and living a godly life."

"And how does this Shaming occur?"

I swallowed hard and remembered the first time I witnessed a Shaming. "They chain the Cursed to the Shaming post. Sometimes they strip him naked. Then the penitents shout insults, sometimes they throw things. They whip the Cursed if he has committed a legal crime. If it is an especially onerous crime, they whip him to death."

He squeezed my hand, and it comforted me that he sympathized with me.

"Why would a *yonsu* allow this to happen to one under his care?"

I shall love this man to death and beyond for uttering that one sentence.

"The Holy Texts say that submitting to Shaming purifies the soul of the Cursed and is a great benefit. A Cursed that submits to Shaming can enter Heaven upon their physical death." My voice sounded bitter even to my ears. What must Kaj think of us?

The cart stopped with a hard jolt that knocked us forward. The crowd was too thick to travel the rest of the road. "Forgive me, *Yonsu*," said the driver. "I cannot go farther."

The man handed Kaj a clipboard, and he looked to me asking with his eyes what he should do.

I was not used to this. My father always knew what to do and provided a model of male strength any man would emulate. But Kaj was a man out of place. He was here with me, ready to face the formidable Thyenn Sharr on my father's behalf. Kaj did not have to do this, and perhaps, because of his position as the earth ambassador, should not.

"Press the ring into this area," I said.

"I have no wax."

"Unnecessary. The paper is a certain kind that will darken at the pressure point."

He did what I instructed and handed back the clipboard.

"Thank you, *Yonsu*," said the driver. He bowed his head. "May fortune find your house and dwell within."

"And your house as well," replied Kaj.

He was always gracious. At that moment, in my distress over my father's fate, I could not have offered a response.

We left the cart, and two Church police appeared out of the throng. What in hell were these two doing here?

"Ambassador," said one. "Most Reverend Sharr sent us to facilitate your arrival."

Anger curled in my gut. Who did Sharr have watching us to know our movements so precisely? A maid new to the household, perhaps?

Kaj gave a small flourish of his hand, pointing toward the church. One guard blew a whistle, and the other held out his hands on either side, forcing an opening in the thick crowd.

Irdrana stood waiting for us on the steps of the church. She was immediately recognizable through the mass of gray robed penitents from her yellow underwrap and red overwrap. She was a beacon of hope in a dark storm, threatening to chase away the gathering gale by her very presence.

I loved my cousin fiercely. She was everything I was not. She was like me, buffeted by a society that does not value her as much as a man. But she stood resolute, brave and fearless in her actions. If they allowed her to be in the civilian or church police force, I was sure she would run either organization.

We reached her, and I would have hugged her if I could.. She'd done so much this day, for my father, and me.

She bowed to Kaj. "Come."

She led us to the portico where solemn-faced guards stood to prevent the passage of penitents, who must traverse the long way around the church. In earlier years, the penitents would walk the portico. But there were many entrances to the church proper here. They tempted penitents to cut through the nave to reach the central courtyard, their first destination on the road to redemption.

But we were not common people, and the guards recognized us. That the members of our house were so well known was another reason Thyenn Sharr hated us.

Irdrana drew us into an alcove in the atrium that housed one of the tall and skinny windows of the church. She placed two sets of documents on the sill.

"Mark these," she said, producing a small wooden box that contained a wax candle and matches. Irdrana dripped the wax on the documents and Kaj, after glancing at me for my approval, set the seal of office for House Klath into them. Irdrana added hers to endorse the documents.

"This one," said Irdrana, holding up one paper. "I will take them to the city clerk's office right now. But here is a copy for you affirming the transfer of House Klath to you, Kaj, should Thyenn Sharr argue with you. But at this point there are enough witnesses that should he make trouble for you on this, it will go badly for him."

"Thank you, Irdrana," I said.

"And this one is the Writ to Show Cause. Once you hand this to the court, Sharr must make a judgment as soon as possible within court hours. Since it is Festival, and it's hell to move around the streets, once you present this to the Court Clerk, do not leave the building. I do not know if he will hear the writ before or after the next scheduled Shaming." She rolled up the remaining papers and stuck them inside the pockets in her overwrap.

She handed me her shoulder bag. "Here is food and drink, should you need it during the wait." She turned her head. "Talm," she called.

A darkly clothed church security guard stepped from the shadows.

She smiled at me. "Talm is a friend, and he'll make sure you get to the Church Court chambers."

"You've thought of everything," I said. I wondered how much Talm's friendship cost.

"Good luck, cousins." Irdrana leaned forward and kissed Kaj's then my cheek hastily then moved off.

"*Yonsu, Yonsa* Klath," said Talm. "Please follow me."

At least the man used the proper forms of address. This measure of respect calmed me a little, but my heart still thumped in my chest as we walked the darkened corridors of the church. This was a place of punishment for my kind, and I recoiled at the horrible memories of what my brothers suffered here.

Talm led us into a chamber in which benches lined the walls.

He pointed to a ledger sitting on a sill by the door. "Enter your names and your business."

"You must do it," said Kaj.

I nodded and entered Kaj's name and the "presentation of Writ To Show Cause Of Imprisonment regarding Aulkus of the House Klath."

Talm pulled a cord dangling by the recess, and the ledger stand rotated one hundred eighty degrees, announcing our arrival to whoever was there to receive it.

"Wait here until someone comes for you. There is no telling how long it will be."

"Thank you, Talm," said Kaj.

I pulled out my wallet from the pocket of my overwrap and offered the man a ten note.

He shook his head. "No, I help for the cause. Thank you for all you are doing, Ambassador." He bowed and walked away.

Kaj sank to one bench. His face had turned that appalling blueish color again.

I sat next to him, worried he was ill. "Kaj?"

"Sorry," he said. "It's all catching up with me. The heat, the gravity." And then he gave me the most amazing grin. "The activity."

Amidst this terrible day, I laughed. That he could do this, lighten my heart in the middle of this mess, caused my heart to open wide. Kaj had not given me any promises, and the future was uncertain, but I knew at that moment I would love him until the end of my days.

What an unholy place to be in to realize you have met the love of your life.

I had settled in my own mind, years ago, that the Faith Progressive Church was a perversion and blasphemy of whatever religion was its original root. There were too many inconsistencies in the holy texts, things that didn't make sense when you analyzed them, to make them a true accounting of the path to enlightenment. This was a heretical thought, subject to judgment and punishment by church leaders. And though my father didn't encourage or discourage my inquiries, when I gave him my thoughts on the subject, he said he always thought the same.

We were heretics, we Klath, a thing that Sharr suspected but could not prove because outwardly we attended services, festivals, and gave yearly tithes to the church. But inwardly we hated it, just as Sharr hated us.

Our views made us hypocrites, but sometimes, my father would say, we may have to suffer a lesser sin, so the greater one doesn't overwhelm us.

"How are you doing?" asked Kaj. He took my hands in his.

"I cannot think or feel. At this moment, I am just trying to put one foot in front of the other."

"I'm sorry you must go through this. This disruption is my fault because your father supported me so thoroughly."

I shook my head. "No, *Yonsu*. Thyenn Sharr has always hated us because my, I mean, our family is more powerful than him. Most Reverend Sharr may have a lock on the religious hearts of Ostakis, but my father wields secular power that Sharr covets. And my father has the support of Mar Seyatt and the city council, another thing that Sharr desires. We are always targets for Sharr. That he tried to diminish us during your installation as Ambassador is a craven attempt to inflame the passions of the people to increase his power."

He put his hand on my shoulder. "You just made the most concise assessment of the situation possible." He looked as if he would say more, but then the double door opened and a seneschal stood at the opening.

"Most Reverend Thyenn Sharr will now hear the petition of the House Klath."

Chapter Fifteen

KAJ

We walked into the darkened room, in which the only light was the sunlight seeping through a large pane of thickened glass to the right. The high church walls strangled the light on all sides of the courtyard shadowing a mass of dark-robed church attendees. In the center, a raised platform dominated the area, and on it was something that sparked a school memory of Earth's deposed theocracy's public punishments.

A pillory.

So they engaged in physical punishment here.

This demonstrated the depths of violence the society tolerated. It was an important consideration going forward in what path my mission took. If I was unsuccessful, the HPC would refuse Ostakis admission to the collective.

The crowd milled, and the discontented faces of the people gathered in the square raised an alarm in me.

Arlan stopped walking halfway up the aisle. "Where is he?"

But I spotted Sharr out the window walking as the crowd parted before him to the raised platform.

"Today," rang the Most Reverend's shrill voice through a speaker set in the wall, "we have a sinner who disobeyed his *yonsu*. He failed to come home at the proper hour and spread his sin throughout the city."

Arlan grabbed my arm. His face lost its color.

Church guards dragged a half-naked man through the crowd that shouted words in anger. "Sinner" seemed to be the most popular word, though I heard "Cursed," and "Begotten from hell." They hauled the young man to the pillory and bent him over it while one guard jerked his arms out to the side and another locked the man in irons. His face had nowhere to go but to rest his chin on the pillory.

Beside me, Arlan let go of my arm, and relaxed. But when he looked at the prisoner again, he breathed a heavy sigh. "Not Pib," he muttered.

The man on the pillory looked terrified. Something about that face was familiar.

"Please," he said. "Please. They threw me out. I had nowhere to go."

It was then I recognized the man who came to my house seeking sanctuary. This was where Silar sent him for care? My gut clenched. Had I known this would happen, I would have given him the refuge he requested, damn my job.

"Liar!" declared Sharr. "Sinner!"

Sharr brought up his hand, and I saw now where he clutched a cat-o'-nine-tails style whip.

"Do you wish to repent your sins, sinner?" said Sharr. "If you admit your guilt, you will not die this day."

The poor man's muscles shook in their restraints. "I repent," he cried. "I have sinned before the lord, and I'm sorry, so very sorry." The man dissolved into tears.

Sharr smiled, though it was one of triumph. "Another sinner will find redemption this day," he proclaimed. The crowd roared its approval, and I shuddered. How could these people be so cruel? The man needed help, not a whipping.

"You shall only have twenty lashes this day for your confession."

Arlan gripped my arm again, and when Sharr laid the first blow to the man, Arlan winced. The man bucked on the pillory, every muscle strained against the pain, and he howled. The crowd cheered.

"Arlan," I said. "Go wait in the hallway. You need not see this."

Arlan pulled away. "No," he said, straightening. "I'm sorry you have to witness this, but you should know. This is what happens to those of my kind. Sharr did not want you to know these things, about us Cursed, about how the Church uses the Lord's name to punish us for who we are."

The beating continued, and I thought Arlan would faint from witnessing the cruelty of Sharr's whip. But though he leaned against me, he didn't say a word as Sharr laid his instrument of punishment, now bloody, into the man's flesh. The man stopped screaming, and his head lolled to the side.

"Is there no one to stop him?" I asked.

"Look at that crowd," said Arlan bitterly. "Do they look like they want him to stop?"

Each blow brought another round of cheers from the crowd. Then Sharr stopped and held up the whip.

"Penance is complete!" he declared.

The crowd roared again, and Sharr walked off the platform as proud as if he was a triumphant performer.

It was sickening.

Sharr got lost in the crowd, but soon a door at the side of the room creaked open.

"Good," he said as he climbed the dais at the end of the aisle. A high desk, like a judges' desk, sat on it. "You're here." An attendant came from the shadows and presented Sharr with a bowl of water, a washcloth, and a towel. Sharr wiped and dried his hands, then stroked his beard with the washcloth.

"Did I get it all?" Sharr calmly asked the attendant.

"Yes, Most Reverend."

"Good." He settled in behind the desk and stared at both of us. "You have business with me?"

"I have a Writ to Show Cause regarding Aulkus Klath."

"And you are what to Aulkus Klath?"

"Nothing," I replied.

"Ah, so. I don't see why you are here."

"I am, however, the *yonsu* of House Klath. Aulkus belongs to House Klath, so I am here to speak for him."

"I heard this from my guard. I do not believe you."

Arlan stepped forward, but I pulled him back. "Please," I murmured. "I can handle this." After witnessing the horror of that man's punishment, I did not want Arlan to fall prey to Sharr.

I turned back to Sharr. "Irdrana Vos filed the papers in the city clerk's office. I'll wait if you want to send someone to confirm it."

Sharr stared at me as if he wanted me to feel his lash. He pawed the Writ to Show Cause and stared at it. He snapped it to the top of his desk.

"Aulkus Klath is a sinner. He refuses to submit his son, Arlan, to Shaming, which by church law he should. If he does not submit Arlan for Shaming, then he will take the punishment."

"No!" cried Arlan.

"You," said Sharr, shaking his finger at Arlan, "incite men to sin. Your parent incited your father to sin, and you continue this with your father's support."

"You can stop that, Sharr," I said. "Stop trying to scare a young man concerned for his father."

"What do you know about it? About our pain that this, this, abomination continues to walk among us."

"Admittedly, very little. But I do know about human decency, Sharr, and here you are showing little."

"Heretic!" he declared.

Yes. This is what Sharr wanted to prove all along. He wanted me off his planet because he knows I represent the Ostakian expanding horizons and a path to the stars. The sooner he could get me gone, the better he would like it.

"I'm not one of your faithful you can intimidate with verses of your sacred text."

"Exactly. You shouldn't be here at all."

"I'm here because of the authority that Aulkus Klath gave me. The sooner you return him to House Klath, the sooner I can give him back the authority that is rightfully his."

Sharr looked at me, then shifted his eyes to Arlan.

"Do you swear that you have not sinned with that one?" He pointed his finger to Arlan, and I swear I wanted to snap the bony thing off his hand.

"His name is Arlan. And no, there is no sin between Arlan Klath and me."

"*Yonsu*," said Arlan. He sounded frightened, and I didn't blame him. Most Reverend Sharr sat in his seat of judgment, with strategically placed spots highlighting his fearsome visage making him seem more powerful than he was.

"What of it, Arlan Klath? Have you committed sin with the Earth Ambassador?"

"Don't say a word, Arlan," I commanded.

"You cannot deceive me," said Sharr. "I've learned you spent a night in your sanctuary room with that Cursed one."

"As you've pointed out, I'm not from here, Sharr. What Arlan and I did is no sin."

"Heretic!" he proclaimed.

"I would be careful, if I were you, Sharr. I am the voice of the homeworld here. What I say determines whether your planet gets the trade for the metals your planet needs to fuel your technological growth."

"Just who do you speak for?" snapped Sharr. "The homeworld or the House Klath? You are the one who must be careful. You tread a direct line to a conflict of interest with your duties as Ambassador and your duties as the *yonsu* of House Klath."

"You let me worry about my duties, Sharr. What can we do to get Aulkus released?"

"Well, there is something else to consider." He looked over his shoulder and addressed someone in the shadows. "Get him."

"What is it you want, Sharr?"

"That is Most Reverend Sharr to you, Ambassador," he said nastily.

"Forgive me," I said. But I couldn't bring myself to speak more of an apology.

"Most Reverend. He is here."

"Bring him forth."

But instead of Aulkus, a young man I hadn't seen before stumbled forward after being shoved by a Church guard.

"Pib!" said Arlan.

"Who is that?"

"My best friend. Cursed like me."

"What do you want, Reverend?" I said darkly. I was beyond patience with the cleric.

"You have a choice. Pib Alluven gained a sentence to the lash for disobeying his *yonsu*. But you can take him or Aulkus home."

"What about his family?" asked Arlan.

"They have disowned him to pursue a path to redemption."

"You mean they handed him to you to kill him," snarled Arlan.

"Tell your Cursed to hold his tongue in this holy court," snapped Sharr.

There was nothing holy in this court. No. Sharr was like other men who had too much power and too little wisdom to handle it. But that he had the power of life and death was frightening.

But I looked at Arlan, and he returned my gaze.

"Our laws protect my father, but not Pib," he said. His voice cracked at the last phrase. What did it cost him to choose his best friend and not his father? It was a hellish choice, and Sharr watched Arlan with delight gleaming in his eyes.

Who was the sinner here?

"Ask him how much money he wants," Arlan whispered with his hands balled into hard fists.

"What will it cost, Sharr, to take both?"

"That's not possible."

"Oh, come now, Sharr. You are the Most Reverend Sharr. You can make it possible."

"Offer your Cursed for Shaming. He's never had one, due to his father's state of sin."

"Kaj," whispered Arlan. I saw in his eyes for his father's sake he would suffer the lash, but that was what his father wished to avoid. It became clear that Aulkus' display of defiance in refusing to submit Arlan to shaming was at the heart of Sharr's power play. Klath's refusal diminished Sharr's power because men like Sharr never liked to have their authority challenged.

Sharr hoped to play on Arlan's emotions and my naïveté. But unlike Sharr, who could only bludgeon others with his power, I knew the art of negotiation.

"No," I said firmly.

My diplomat father taught me some things are negotiable, and others are not. Aulkus handed me the authority of House Klath because he expected me to protect it and Arlan. The last thing I wanted was to play into the hands of this megalomaniac. Sharr had overplayed his hand.

"Come along, Arlan, Pib," I said. I began my walk down the aisle.

"You'll regret this," yelled Sharr.

I could not resist. Marta got embarrassed when I showed my pique. She had counseled me repeatedly about acting above it all. But sometimes I could not resist, and this day, after being pushed hard, I could not.

So I turned and faced the Most Reverend Sharr. "I already do. But by the time I'm done, you will have regretted meeting me much more. Good day, Reverend Sharr. We'll see each other again soon."

And with that, I strode out of Sharr's seat of justice, and out of this church of the damned with Arlan and his friend following me.

Chapter Sixteen

ARLAN

I was in shock. No one spoke to Reverend Sharr the way my *yonsu* did. When we got out of the church, Kaj turned to me.

"Are you okay?" he asked.

His first thought was for me. I felt my cheeks flush. I was not used to anyone other than my father caring for how I felt. "Yes, *Yonsu.*"

Pib stared at my Kaj with a mixture of adoration and shock. "*Yonsu*—how can I thank you?"

"Thank Arlan. He wanted to make sure you were safe."

"But Trademaster Klath—"

"He knew well enough the danger he was in."

Kaj started down the steps expecting us to follow. The crowd parted as he moved toward the street, his purposeful steps provided all the authority needed to clear his own way. Pib and I exchanged looks.

"Gentlemen," he said, calling up to us. And we hurried down.

"Wow," said Pib. "I can see why you love him. I think I'm in love with him myself."

My jaw clenched. This was not the time for one of Pib's jokes. Nor did I like the way he glanced at my *yonsu*. But the problem was Kaj was my *yonsu* in name only. Kaj made no promises. He made that clear.

Kaj stood at the curb as if he expected an electric cart to arrive, and to my astonishment, one did.

"In you go, both of you," he said. He sat in the front seat while Pib and I took the back. The driver drove the cart into the crowd surrounding the church, and they parted. I looked back at the hulking architecture of the Faith Progressive Church with dread. My father was still in there, and I could only hope the guards did not mistreat him. I couldn't be sure after Thyenn Sharr reminded all of us of the cruelty in his heart. The face of the man Sharr whipped burned in my soul, and my heart curled at the thought of Sharr flogging Pib to death. My father will understand my decision when he hears of this.

"Arlan," Kaj said. "When we get home, I want you to write a report about the number of dollars House Klath has generated in the past year. Project how much money each day Aulkus brings in."

"*Yonsu*?" I asked. This was a strange request.

"I assume there is a civil court that hears damage claims? I believe your father talked about such a thing?"

"Yes, *Yonsu*."

"My mother was a lawyer. Her favorite saying was that the only place to seek real justice was in a civil court. If the Faith Progressive Church insists on holding your father, I will sue them for damages for loss of business while they jail him.

"I'm glad we could rescue your friend. But Sharr did not respond to our writ. This is bad faith on the Church Court's part, and if your courts are anything like the homeworld, that should support a motion in the civil court."

"I wouldn't know, *Yonsu*. I only know the laws that relate to accounting business books."

"We should talk to a solicitor then," said Kaj.

"Tell the driver to pull up to that kiosk."

Kaj gave the directive, and the driver stopped at a messenger service kiosk. There were several messenger services, but this was one my father favored for House business, so we had an account with them.

"Wait for us," said Kaj firmly to the driver, who nodded. The man who attended the kiosk was a Cursed. I finally understood why my father used this service above others, for he supported those businesses that gave gainful employment to the Cursed.

"*Yonsu*?" The man looked up at Kaj, who smiled at him. I was glad others recognized Kaj as a *yonsu* and it caused my heart to swell with pride.

"We need a pen and paper," I said. "And then we need the message delivered today, as soon as possible."

"Yes, exactly," affirmed Kaj.

The man handed us the paper and pen, and I looked at Kaj.

"What do you want me to say, *Yonsu*?"

"Address it to your father's solicitor and ask him to come to our house as soon as possible. Tell him it is an urgent matter."

I wrote out the note and the attendant had the wax ready. Kaj pressed the ring into the wax.

"Oh," said the attendant excitedly when he saw the seal. "House Klath. Yes, *Yonsu*, it will go out immediately." He snapped his fingers, and a younger man came from the shadows of the portico of the building where the kiosk sat.

"Urgent," he said.

The young man, after looking at the address, took off running down toward the Church Point area. Even I was surprised by this level of service.

"Is there a bill I need to mark?" Kaj asked the attendant.

"No, sir. Not for House Klath. Not today. And we thank you, *Yonsu*, for all that your House is doing for us this day."

"I don't understand what you mean."

"Word's gone out, sir, of how House Klath refuses to let the Church Shame their Cursed, and that Aulkus Klath sits in the Church jail. And that you, Yonsu, stood up to Thyenn Sharr"—he spat onto the street after saying his name—"in Sharr's own Holy Court. We did not know how the Earth Ambassador would look upon us. But many people in Kiji Ost now think favorably on the Earth Ambassador. The word's gone out to all the cities, that joined in purpose is House Klath and the House of the Earth Ambassador."

Kaj frowned then. And why should he not? He was the Earth Ambassador and should not be in the middle of our society's upset. "You can tell whoever you wish that the Earth Ambassador wants nothing more than the happiness of the Ostakian people."

The man bowed. "Yes, *Yonsu*. I will say so."

We traveled the rest of the way home in silence. Kaj appeared deep in thought. Pib looked stricken.

"Your father is in prison?" he whispered in shock.

"Yes. That is why Kaj is acting as our *yonsu*."

"He seems so natural as one."

Yes, he was. And I wondered at this. Were all men from Earth like this? With the ability to command respect just with his presence?

We pulled up to the house, and Edemar greeted us. "*Yonsu, Yonsa*, and *Syad* Pib. I am glad to see you return," he said as we entered the atrium.

Kaj nodded. "Thank you, *Rasee Yinsi* Edemar."

"How is *Yonsu* Klath?" Edemar asked.

"Sharr wouldn't let us see him." There was bitterness in Kaj's voice. "Instead he sent Pib home with us."

"*Syad* Pib?"

He looked away. "I am no longer welcome in my parent's home."

I threw my arm around Pib. "You are welcome here."

"If your *yonsu* says."

"I so say," said Kaj.

"*Yonsu*," said Edemar, "This house has visitors."

"Who?"

"Ambassador Irdrana Vos and *Yon* Ushos Phale. The Ambassador is in the study. *Yon* Phale is in the dining room."

"And who is *Yon* Phale to this house?" Kaj asked.

"He is one of Master Klath's assistants," said Edemar.

"And the person I am contracted with," I said.

Kaj's jaw stiffened, and his eyes narrowed. "What does he want?" Kaj asked Edemar.

"I did not ask."

"Come with me, Arlan." Kaj strode to the dining room. Edemar had to run to catch up to open the door for Kaj.

Ushos stood immediately. "Arlan, I came as soon as I heard. If you wish, we can dispense with the mating until—"

"Who are you again?" Kaj asked.

"I am Arlan's contracted partner."

"Arlan?" Kaj's voice was cold with anger. "Do you want this man?"

"No, I do not."

"We appreciate your offer to become Arlan's *yonsu*," said Kaj. "But not needed. Aulkus Klath assigned authority of House Klath to me and he is mine to care for."

Ushos' eyes went wide. "What do you mean, yours to care for?" Ushos asked with suspicion in his eyes. "House Phale and House Klath contracted an agreement."

"The Agreement is off," said Kaj.

"But I was to get the seals of authority for House Klath," he snapped.

Kaj's eyes narrowed as if he suspected Ushos of performing a foul deed.

"*Yonsu* Klath gave me the ring and signed papers making me yonsu of House Klath. An associate filed the papers in the City Clerk's office. So what are you doing here?"

"Asserting my rights. You can't come in here and take over. You aren't even a citizen."

"Ushos," I said, "you failed to finish the payments on the contract. Thus it is not complete, and the *Yonsu* of House Klath can negate it."

"Did he touch you?" said Ushos in a threatening voice.

"That is none of your business," said Kaj.

"This is outrageous!" yelled Ushos. "I will see you in court."

"You are welcome to. *Rasee Yinsi*, please see *Yon* Phale to the door."

"Come, *Yon* Phale."

"This isn't right. Arlan is mine," he spat.

"We'll refund the sums at the earliest convenience," I said, and probably too happily. The idea of being with Ushos Phale sickened me now.

Kaj stared at Ushos as he left through the front door and did not break his gaze until the door shut.

"That is who you chose?" Kaj asked unhappily, folding his arms across his chest.

"No," I said. "Ushos has been after me for some time to consummate the contract, but I wouldn't. But why are you questioning me? You told me you could make no promises to me."

Kaj jerked his head up as if I struck him. "Yes, I said that."

"And can you? Would you?"

"I, I don't know. I'm supposed to forge relations with Ostakis."

"Mission accomplished," I said snottily. "If you've gotten me with a child, you've affiliated yourself with the most powerful house on Ostakis. If you don't stay with me and be my *yonsu*, I'll have the child, and have no need to make a partnership again. Hell, I can whore myself on the streets. Not a single person could say a thing about it because I fulfilled my role and brought a new generation to House Klath."

My words were bitter and unnecessarily so. But in a short time, too short of one, I'd fallen for Kaj Deder. The idea he would leave me rent my heart in a thousand pieces.

"Arlan." The pain was evident in his voice and his face. But what reason did Kaj have to hurt? He had me, and enjoyed himself, and sometimes that was all we Cursed expected. I was lucky in that my house provided money and social standing for whoever would partner with me, but many of my kind didn't have that luxury. Maybe this thing with Kaj was my punishment for taking what I had and who I was for granted. I may be Cursed, but I lived a better life than many people in this city.

Pib came to the door and stood stock still, taking in the charged atmosphere between Kaj and me.

"How about daymeal? Eh? I'm starving." He said this as jovially as he could, but I wasn't in the mood. I had eaten nothing all day, but my stomach was a lead weight, and thinking of food sickened me.

"Please do me a favor and ask Ija to put together something for the household. I have a task my *yonsu* gave me to do."

"Arlan," said Kaj again.

I heard the plea in his voice, but I ignored it. "It's best if you don't talk to me for a while."

Chapter Seventeen

KAJ

I needed a moment to think. Events were moving much too swiftly, and the sense I had a grip on things was fast slipping from me.

So many questions flooded my brain, I had to sit down, which I did at the long table meant to stage enormous dinner parties.

Arlan explained he was one of the "Cursed," and at first I assumed it was an invective against his sexual orientation. And in all matters except for the curious fluid that leaked from his entrance, he seemed thoroughly male. But the news he could get pregnant shocked me.

Human behavior is remarkably consistent despite us having settled hundreds of worlds in the past thirty centuries. When the first contact team arrived and inserted itself in Ostakian society, it noted elements that were distinct aberrations of human behavior. Patriarchy we understood, though that it flourished disappointed us. But what was not, was that some young men seemed to suffer as much as women, and this was not normal. Now I understood the discrimination against those with the biology of the Cursed. How and why these genetic mutations arose out of the human male/female paradigm was the question. And it was my job to find out.

Truthfully, I was more of a spy than an ambassador, though right now all my objectivity was out the window. There was no way I could write a report that could show Thyenn Sharr in a neutral light.

But I would have to make my peace with my supervisor, who circled in orbit behind the Ostakian moon, another time. She would leave in the HPC vessel in another twenty days. In the ship, she had the manpower to perform the insertions of homeworld personnel to colony planets. It was a heavy schedule, five planets to visit in their lifetime, insert the observation and first contact teams, gather information, devise a contact plan and implement it. Then they would travel to the next destination to do it again.

Behind that ship, a year out was one with replacement personnel and supplies.

And me?

That was why I was here. I trained for the risky first ambassadorial post, and it was my job to prepare Ostakis for entrance into the HPC. We were all well aware that my actions most likely would cause my death.

A hollow knock at the door reverberated through the atrium, and I looked up as Edemar opened the door.

"Come in, *Yonsu* Solicitor," said the *rasee yinsee.*

"My house is pleased to visit this one once more. Where might I find the young *yonsu*?"

"He's in the dining room, *Yonsu.*"

"No need," I said, standing. "We can go to the office."

"You can, *yonsu.* Should I delay daymeal then?"

My stomach rumbled as I remembered I hadn't eaten since yesterday.

"No. Please have the food brought in the dining room and ask Ambassador Vos to join us."

"Very good, *Yonsu.*"

Edemar bowed, and I beckoned the solicitor of House Klath into the dining room. He stood the same height as Aulkus, the top of his head coming to my chin, and he had a broad chest.

"My House is honored to serve yours, Trademaster Klath."

"My House is honored that you serve us. Please, my name is Kaj. I've not had the honor of learning yours."

"Tenden Hauk, Solicitor, Civil, and Church certified."

"Solicitor Hauk," said Irdrana as she entered the dining room. "My House is pleased to meet yours again."

"The lovely Irdrana. And when will you accept that invitation for a moonlight ride on Lake Veller?"

Irdrana laughed. "You are a rascal, Tenden Hauk." Her voice was light, but the consternation her eyes spoke was the truth. She did not appreciate this most inappropriate turn in the conversation.

Maybe my expression conveyed my thoughts because Irdrana spoke to me directly. "House Hauk is the best of their profession in Kiji Ost, and House Klath has used his family's services for several generations."

"Three," said Hauk with a smile. "We have a long association with House Klath."

"Please, sit, both of you. We need to discuss Aulkus' situation."

"*Yonsu,*" said an older woman, "may we enter and serve the daymeal?"

I nodded, feeling a touch disoriented since I could not place her name though I had met her earlier. Exhaustion hit me then, from the long day, and the heat and gravity, and I sank to my seat.

Irdrana, who sat on my right side patted my hand.

"Are you feeling unwell, Kaj?" she asked with concern in her eyes.

I shook my head.

"Ah, Ija," said Hauk. "How is the best cook in Kiji Ost?"

"Quite happy with my duties here at House Klath," said Ija with a frown. She and two other women hurriedly set the table and poured wine as they served the daymeal.

"You must pay her well, Klath. She has turned down my offers of employment several times."

This was my solicitor? I only hoped his skill as a lawyer exceeded his manners. In my short time here, Aulkus had spoiled me with an excess of proficiency in all things, both in him and the people who worked for him. The proof of it was in the meal before me. Ija had prepared a meal that had no meat. On my plate sat a slice of quiche, a salad, and a cup of vegetable soup. The woman learned my preferences quickly. I was sure there was no need to pull out the food analyzer, which I must have misplaced.

"Thank you, Ija, for this lovely meal."

"You are most welcome, *Yonsu*."

"Tell me, Ija. Who is the most recent addition to your staff?"

"That is Senesea, here."

"Senesea."

"Yes, *Yonsu*."

"Are you a pious woman?"

"Yes, *Yonsu*. I praise the Lord and all his holy works."

"And Reverend Sharr?"

She looked nervously from me to Ija. "What of Reverend Sharr?"

"Do you take his words most seriously?"

"Yes, *Yonsu*."

"So if Most Reverend Sharr asked you to spy on this household?"

"I don't know what you mean," she said nervously.

"If Reverend Sharr said it was a holy thing to pass reports of what happens in this household to him, would you do it?"

"I, I," stammered the unfortunate Senesea.

"You're relieved of your position on this staff. Gather your possessions and depart immediately."

"*Yonsu*," she started. Obviously, she intended to make a plea. I would not listen to it.

"Ija, make sure the young lady departs immediately."

"As you wish, *yonsu*."

Ija and the servants with her bowed and left the room. Senesea made some vague protests as Ija led her out, but all that faded as they drew away.

"Please eat. We'll dispense with the prayer of thanks for the meal this time."

Irdrana smiled. "Of course, *Yonsu*. House Klath has many concerns this day."

"What do you know about our situation, Hauk?" I asked.

"What all Ostakis knows. That Aulkus Klath sits in the jail at the Church and you did not secure his release upon the Writ to Show Cause I wrote earlier this day."

I nodded. "Thyenn Sharr refused to consider the petition."

"That is a serious charge."

"Arlan was with him," said Irdrana. "He'll witness to the events."

"It is no secret in this city that Thyenn Sharr is jealous of House Klath's secular power. But if he refuses to release Klath there is little we can do."

"I don't agree," I replied. "Aulkus Klath is a significant asset to House Klath. Thyenn Sharr discharged his duties incompetently and in doing so has harmed House Klath financially."

Hauk leaned forward in his chair with interest written on his face. "That sounds like the framing of a legal argument."

"It is. For the civil court."

"And what do you hope to gain by this?"

"I do not know how Ostakis practices law, but on Earth, the threat of a civil lawsuit is enough to leverage a position for negotiation."

"It is a stunning proposal," said Hauk. He pursed his lips. "But Thyenn Sharr offers alternatives in his Holy Court. The civil court might not hear your petition on that ground saying that redress was possible at that time."

"He offered a deal. But the terms were unacceptable. He proposed to Shame either Aulkus or Arlan, and I won't have that."

"You won't?" said Hauk incredulously. "I tell you, you are taking the hard way on this. The civil court does not like to hear suits against the Church."

"And I said the threat of a lawsuit gives us the chance of a serious negotiation. I said nothing about letting the suit get to court."

Hauk tapped his fingers on the table, another rudeness, while he considered my words. "And how do you intend on proving a financial loss?"

"Arlan, right now, is calculating the money Aulkus brings into House Klath. There is enough history to make a claim his loss to the house represents a significant hardship."

"I see," said Hauk.

I was growing annoyed with Hauk's attitude. Why was he reluctant?

"Can you write the suit or not?" I spoke sharply enough that Irdrana jerked her head up from her food.

"You have to understand. Thyenn Sharr—"

"Leave us," I said. "Your services are no longer needed by House Klath."

The solicitor's face grew red and he sputtered. "You can't do that."

"Yes. I can." I pulled the silken cord behind me. "Edemar, please see Solicitor Hauk to the door. And he won't be coming back."

With a rude huff, Hauk rose from the table.

"And I expect your office to deliver all recent files relating to House Klath as soon as possible," I added.

"I'll have them copied. It will take several days."

"You'll deliver the originals, all of them," I said. "Today."

"This will cost you, Klath. You do not know the sands you travel."

"Perhaps I don't," I replied. "But I'll make my way faster without people blocking my way."

Edemar saw the solicitor to the door and returned. "Is there anything else you wish, *Yonsu*?"

"No. Yes. The messenger service House Klath uses. There is a kiosk close to the church, and an elderly man works it. Ask that he comes here as soon as he is able. Whatever his time is worth, pay him."

"Yes, *Yonsu*."

Edemar rushed off to complete this latest task.

Irdrana arched an eyebrow. "Do you intend to discharge anyone else from the service of House Klath today?"

"Anyone who is not absolutely loyal to it, yes. Aulkus' life hangs in the balance, and I cannot risk it further because people don't know where the wind blows."

"It seems people think that the wind blows for Thyenn Sharr."

"They are wrong," I replied. "If this planet is to grow economically then it needs to trade with the Human Planets Collective, not follow Sharr's regressive policies. Which Sharr knows. His only chance to retain his power is to grab the Trademaster position. He failed on his first try. He won't stop trying."

"It seems you have strayed from your position as ambassador."

"I did not ask to head House Klath, but I'll be damned if I let a bigoted, small-minded megalomaniac take control of this planet."

"You sound more like an operative than an ambassador now."

"I still work for the interests of the Human Planets Collective, Irdrana. And it is not in our interests that Thyenn Sharr gains total control. We decided in our mission design that Thyenn Sharr can keep his position as the head of the Faith Progressive Church. But he cannot gain any more power than that. We won't deal with him."

"So," said another voice from the doorway. "You've been playing games with us from the beginning."

I looked up to see Arlan standing there. "And what am I? Another game piece? Screw the Cursed of House Klath and gain a better position?"

"Arlan." I jerked my head toward the office door across the atrium. "Excuse me, Irdrana. Arlan and I will have a little talk."

Chapter Eighteen

ARLAN

My heart pounded as Kaj brought me into my father's, now his, office. But instead of sitting behind the desk as my father would, he shut the door and stood in front of me. He looked almost frightened, as if he was the one who had been incalculably rude and deserved punishment.

"Listen, Arlan. You are right. Irdrana is correct. I am more than an ambassador, though I would have played it that way if the Faith Progressive Church did not have as much power as they do."

"Played it?" I started.

He put his finger to my lips. "Please, Arlan. Hear me out first. Our first team died here, killed by religious extremists. We got little information only because of that volatile situation. One out of ten ambassadors trained as I did, and I only took that training after my wife—"

"Wife? You have a wife?" The floor swirled under me. What have I gotten into? Pib's plight flashed through my mind and for a second, I imagine myself in that same wretched situation.

"Arlan, I took this job *after* my wife died."

I stared at him horrified, both at his loss and my stupid insensitivity.

"I'm sorry for your loss, but I don't understand."

"My official title is High-Risk Operative. The HPC sends people with my training into ambassadorial positions when they judge the situation too dangerous for standard personnel."

My breath hitched. "Too dangerous? As in life threatening?"

He nodded. "My job is to evaluate this society and make Ostakis ready for admission into the Human Planets Collective."

"And how will you do that? I don't understand how that threatens your life."

"It all depends on how things shake out the next few days. The HPC won't stand for Thyenn Sharr to control Ostakis. So the only hope for Ostakis is if I can get Sharr to back down. Otherwise, the people of Ostakis will descend into a rigid religious patriarchy, and those, we've found over time, are dangerous entities. If that happens, then we cannot allow Ostakis passage to the stars."

I swallowed hard as the import of Kaj's words hit me.

"You mean that we must survive on our dwindling resources. And when those go, we'll fail as a society."

"Yes. We estimate that all human life on Ostakis will die off in less than a thousand years."

"And you'll allow that?"

"It isn't up to me, Arlan. It's the result that counts. If Thyenn Sharr's power play for House Klath fails, then Ostakis will gain admission to the HPC. If he gets control, then we can't allow a fundamental religious sect access to the stars."

"Kaj." I spoke in a strangled voice. "What would you do to stop Sharr?"

"Whatever it takes, Arlan."

I blinked. "Whatever?"

"Listen, the stakes are too high here. The reason that Earth lost contact with the colony worlds is that a fundamentalist religious group seized control of much of the planet. Governments dissolved under their influence. The Church ran the planet, subjecting people to inhumane laws."

"Like Thyenn Sharr does."

"Yes. We only in the past five hundred years gained our freedoms back. The HPC is very cautious about letting such groups into the collective. We do not want a repeat of the last twenty-five hundred years."

"And you think Thyenn Sharr is that much of a threat, not only to Ostakis but the whole human race?"

"We won't give him a chance to find out."

"And if you do not recommend Ostakis' inclusion in the HPC, will you go back to Earth?"

He touched my cheek. "Arlan, I can never go back to Earth. I told you, the Earth on which I lived died five hundred years ago. No. If after I complete my assignment, if I'm still alive, I'll go with the HPC ship in orbit to the next mission."

"Your ship is still in orbit? I thought it left."

"We give that impression to let events play out naturally. Once I go back, or if they don't get a signal to retrieve me, which means I'm dead, the ship will leave. A year from now, the second ship will arrive with the real ambassador."

"You never intended to stay, did you?" Tears misted my eyes.

"Arlan," he said, and his voice broke. "I told you. I am a High-Risk Operative. Most people in my position don't survive their mission."

Now my heart thundered and I finally got it. Kaj, my beautiful Kaj, offered himself for a suicide mission because of his loss and grief over his wife's death. My hand moved reflexively to my stomach as if protecting something. Or someone.

Was I with child? It was too soon to tell. Still, the possibility existed, and how could we survive without our *yonsu*?

"You-you," I said, stuttering. "You promised to support my decisions."

"I did, and I do."

"But how can you do that if you are dead or gone?"

"I will do everything I can to bring your father home."

"Damn it, Kaj. That's not what I mean."

But a rap on the door cut the discussion short.

"Come in," said Kaj.

"*Yonsu*," said Edemar, "the Cursed you asked for is at the door."

"Bring him to the dining room and bring a fresh plate of the daymeal, and one for Arlan too."

"Very good, *Yonsu*." Edemar shut the door again.

"I can't eat," I said.

"You will eat, Arlan. You're upset and with good reason. But you cannot help our child or me if you don't nourish yourself."

"I don't know if I'm pregnant."

Kaj opened the door. "I do," he said with finality. "Come."

I followed Kaj wondering how he was so sure of something I was not. I sat next to Irdrana who sensibly had finished her meal. Things were moving too quickly to wait for the chance to eat again.

Edemar brought the man from the kiosk who helped us with the message to the solicitor and announced him as Serren of House Mem.

"Sit," said Kaj.

Serren sat at the gleaming dark-wood table hundreds of years old with an expression of astonishment on his face. His mouth opened in surprise when Ija brought two more plates of food.

"Here," said Kaj. "Have my wine. I have not drunk from it."

"*Yonsu*, you overwhelm me."

"We have little time so let me get to business. I'm sure you know all the people in the city who support your cause."

"My cause, *Yonsu*?"

"Equal treatment for the Cursed."

"*Yonsu*," he protested.

"Do not be frightened. I want to help you. But first I need your assistance. I need the name of a solicitor, certified in civil and church forms to help draft and deliver a lawsuit."

"*Yonsu*?"

"He must be someone who is not afraid of Thyenn Sharr."

"Thyenn Sharr frightens all of us. But there are one or two that would give their lives to protect the Cursed. How will your lawsuit do that?"

"Make him and the Church responsible for the financial losses of House Klath by imprisoning Aulkus Klath who produces our income."

Serren clapped his hands in delight. "How clever, *Yonsu*. I know just the man."

"Then send for him."

"Certainly, *Yonsu*. One of my runners waits outside."

Serren excused himself and opened the front door. He spoke in excited tones to whoever stood outside and then returned.

"A half-hour, *Yonsu*, no more."

"Enjoy the daymeal."

Within thirty minutes another knock brought the gentleman to the door. Edemar introduced him as Malden Tyre. He agreed quickly to write the document and Kaj instructed him to sit in the office and draft it.

"I will have this thing on Sharr's desk before nightfall," said Kaj in a determined voice. "Do you have the figures, Arlan?"

"Yes, *Yonsu.*"

"Then, please, give them to *Yonsu* Solicitor."

"As you wish, *Yonsu.*"

"Will you not call me Kaj at home?" he asked.

I lowered my eyes. I had treated Kaj horribly with my temper when all he had done was help my house, my father, me, and Pib. Even if he left me, I owed him my respect.

"Whatever you want, Kaj."

I gave Tyre the figures plus currency notes for a deposit on his work. I would send him a draft for the rest later.

Kaj stood at the doorway with his arms folded. "House Klath needs a new solicitor. If you can do the work, we may give you a retainer."

"Yes, *Yonsu.*" The man's eyes gleamed with appreciation. A client like House Klath would improve his standing immeasurably.

Irdrana came to the office when the man finished, looked over the document and nodded her approval. And with a round of signatures and seals, Kaj's, Irdrana's, and Tyre's, the lawsuit was ready.

"I will deliver this to the Holy Court personally, *Yonsu,*" said Tyre. His eyes gleamed with appreciation, and I knew my *yonsu* made a fast friend this day.

Tyre and Serren exited in noisy conversation, and Irdrana took her leave.

"I hope this works," said Irdrana at the door.

"If it shakes up Sharr and brings him to a more reasonable frame of mind so he releases Aulkus, then we will have done well. I will take the next steps."

Irdrana kissed me, then glanced at Kaj. "Take care of my cousin, *Yonsu* Klath. He deserves a good man like you."

"I will do everything I can."

I died a little at those words. Kaj would do what he could as long as he was here on Ostakis. But he could just as easily leave.

Or die.

Irdrana bowed and left, and with her absence, silence settled in the house.

Kaj put his arm around me and kissed the top of my head. "I wish there was a safer place for you since I fear I will be the target of Sharr's wrath and make you one too."

"You shouldn't worry about me. Sharr has always made me his target. This is nothing new."

"We should rest."

I could see how tired Kaj was. The day wore on him.

"You rest. I will check on Pib."

"Then come to my bed quickly. Wait, what bed is mine anyway?"

"How about my room?" I suggested. "I will put Pib in one of the guest rooms."

Kaj nodded, and I joined Pib in my office.

"How are you doing, Pib?" I asked.

"I'm fine. It settles my mind to work on numbers."

"I'll ask Ija to give you a room. If will be one of the guest rooms close to mine."

"How can I thank you?" asked Pib.

"If I had a brother, I would have wished him to be you, Pib."

"You know, this will not work out."

"What do you mean?"

"Since my family kicked me out, I have no legal standing."

"House Klath employs you. That's all the standing you need."

That was not quite true, but I wanted it to be so. When things resolved for my father, we would formalize Pib's status.

I left Pib to his work, glad someone could work on the accounts since I was too nervous for my father to work. After speaking to Ija about Pib, I found Kaj in my bed, already stripped of his wraps.

"I'm sorry," he said. "It is hot in here."

"That's the worst seduction I've ever heard."

He gave me a grin full of incredulity. "How many seductions have you heard?"

"Too many," I said dramatically as I dropped to my bed.

"What a wanton man you are."

He hooked his arms around me and drew me to him. His strong arms pressing me against him stirred me. I laid my head on his shoulder and kicked off my sandals.

"I thought you wanted to rest," I said.

"What I want is a few minutes with you without the world intruding."

I turned to face him. He was under the sheets, and I on top, and the thought occurred to me that despite everything today I wanted that to change.

"One world," I said, tracing his jaw with my hand. Already his day's stubble had grown and bristled on the tip of my fingers sending sparks through me, "when you have so many worlds you could go to."

His body stiffened at my words.

"Let's not talk of that."

"What shall we talk of then?"

"What I have to say needs no words."

Chapter Nineteen

KAJ

Our lovemaking was sweet instead of the frantic coupling of last night. Afterwards, we fell asleep in each other's arms as if we hadn't a care in the world. But we had problems, and they intruded in the cruelest of ways.

I woke to frantic knocking on the door.

"*Yonsu, Yonsu.*" Panic scored Edemar's voice. But despite his distress, the man wouldn't open the door.

How strangely and incongruously polite these people were. In my head, a little scene played out. "Master, the house is burning down. Please be so kind as to rise from your bed so that I might save you."

"I'm awake," I said loudly. And Arlan woke too.

I got out of bed, pulling the sheet to wrap around my body. Arlan scrambled out of bed and handed me a robe from his closet. It was too small, but at least it covered the necessities. He put one on also.

I opened the door. "What is the problem, Edemar?"

"*Yonsu,* Thyenn Sharr is denouncing you from the pulpit."

I expected that. I didn't see the problem. Edemar recognized too that I didn't.

"*Yonsu,* he calls you unredeemable and declares you banished."

More nonsense words. But Arlan's face morphed from concern to the same panicked look that Edemar wore.

"Come watch," the *ransee yinsi* said. He handed me a larger robe that nearly came to the floor. Amid disaster, the first thing the man thought of was my comfort. So I shed the smaller one to put on the larger. It would not do, it seemed, to face danger showing your legs.

Arlan followed behind closely as Edemar brought me to the kitchen. Ija and the kitchen staff gathered around the holo-emitter watching a miniature Sharr thumping his hand on the pulpit in which he stood.

"The Unbeliever brings his own sin to Ostakis, his willful disregard of God's holy word! He lies with a Cursed. Yes! I saw this with my own eyes how the Earth Ambassador and the son of the sinner, Aulkus Klath, stood before me unrepentant. This while the Earth Ambassador's mark was displayed on the man's skin. But they both denied that they sinned. Before me, the Earth Ambassador lied! Lies! And sin! This is what the representative of the homeworld brings us. And he dared to stand before me as the *yonsu* of House Klath! All he says are lies and defies the Holy Word. We must drive him out, away from Ostakis and bring purity to us once again."

I sighed and shook my head.

"Yonsu," said Arlan. "Is the ship watching this transmission?"

I closed my eyes. "Yes," I said hoarsely.

"What will happen? What will they do?"

"Watch, Arlan. They will watch what the people of Ostakis do."

"But what about you? Won't they send a ship for you?"

"No," I said.

"But you are in danger."

I drew a deep breath and put my arms around my lover's shoulders. His eyes shone at me with so much love my heart nearly burst. What I would do to stay with this man until the end of time? But I had a job I must follow to the end. The fate of Ostakis rested on me.

"And I've told you, Arlan, that I am expendable."

"No!" he cried.

In the background, we heard the cries of agreement to Sharr's unholy proposal from the crowd.

"I demand that Kaj Deder present himself to the Church! This ambassador is an unholy sinner, a craven demon. Kaj Deder, if you do not present yourself here, I will Shame Aulkus Klath for your crimes against the church."

Even I saw that Sharr's reasoning was faulty. In calling me my Earth name, he denied my position as *yonsu* of House Klath. But by demanding Aulkus take my "punishment" affirmed my position as *yonsu* of the house. However, reason did not rule this day.

Church guards dragged Aulkus Klath to the Shaming Post and chained him to it. He had suffered some abuse already for he was bleeding from the side of his head, and his eyes were glassy.

That bastard Sharr. Now I desired to hurt the man. But this was also the moment of decision for which the HPC waited. The conditions were ripe, and my final instructions fit the parameters of what happened now. What I would do would seem perfectly logical and protecting of a key citizen. How the people of Ostakis reacted would determine if Ostakis ultimately lived or died.

"Where are my clothes?" I asked Edemar. "My Earth clothes."

"I will bring them, *Yonsu*."

"No, Kaj," said Arlan. Desperation permeated his voice.

"I will not allow him to further harm your father."

"He won't let you stop him."

"Oh, I'll stop him if I have to kill the man myself."

"What?" Arlan looked shocked. He never conceived of such a thing, and I adored him for it. His heart did not bear the taint of violence or hate despite the abuse he suffered by his own society. Arlan was exactly the type of citizen the HPC desired. As our child would be.

I would make sure of it.

"It was what I trained to do, Arlan. It's the HPC's final solution to save a planet from itself." Arlan continued to stare at me in shock. "It is why they never expected me to return."

"*Yonsu,*" said Edemar, bringing the pile of my clothing I left behind.

I saw the glint of gold on my collar, the HPC insignia pin for the diplomatic service we all wore. There is one thing I can do, and perhaps it is the last action I can perform to protect Arlan. I pulled the HPC pin from my collar and affixed it next to the clasp on the shoulder of his overwrap.

"Wear that and remember me."

"Kaj," he said. His voice broke, but before he could say more, I kissed him, long and hard. The man had to know I loved him from that kiss. But time grew short, and I pulled away with a lump in my throat.

"All of you get into the sanctuary room and lock that door."

"Kaj!" said Arlan in anguish. "I will go with you."

"No," I said firmly. Then to Edemar, I gave my last instruction. "Protect *Yonsa* Arlan. He carries my child."

"I do not know I am pregnant," protested Arlan.

"Then you are the only one," said Ija. "No one's heat lasts only a single night if you are not."

Arlan blushed, and I bent and kissed his cheek.

"You must protect yourself, my love, for all our sakes."

"*Yonsa* Arlan," said Edemar as he laid his hand on Arlan's shoulder. "Let us do as *Yonsu* Kaj asks."

Ija shooed everyone but me from the kitchen, and I heard a heavy door shut. From what I had seen, the Sanctuary room was a vault, and I hoped that was true. At least it now held the treasures of my heart.

As I dressed, I prepared myself mentally for what I was to do. There was no weapon I carried but my training, and that would have to be enough when I faced Thyenn Sharr. The odds were that I would die in this encounter, for Sharr would have many around him who would take me down if I succeeded in murder.

But all I had to remember was the images of the dead First Contact crew—men and women I knew personally. I trained with them in some classes, shared meals and recreation before they left on the survey ship. Though I tried to put a wall around my heart, to not care, for ultimately I was expendable, and they were not, I did. And their deaths angered me.

But the thought of Aulkus on the Shaming post, and the threat to Arlan and my child he carried angered me more. I, who lost my family over and over, first my parents and then my wife, wanted more than anything to keep these people safe.

I wondered how I would get to the Church but found I need not have worried about that when I opened the front door. An electric cart sat there with a driver and the messenger concierge, Serren Mem.

"*Yonsu,* my house is happy to render you service this day," said Serren jauntily. "Come, this is my cousin Josin, and he offered his taxi for your use."

"How did you know I would go to the Church?"

"Why would I think you would not? You have much to settle with the Faith Progressive Church, do you not Earth Ambassador? How their clerics treat your House?

"The Holy Book," he continued, "tells us to love our enemies, but I find that it is easier to love your enemies when they are out of the way." He grinned at me widely, and I saw that in Serren Mem I met a kindred spirit.

"You have an interesting take on Holy Writ, do you not, *Syad* Mem?"

"No more interesting than I suppose you do, *Yonsu* Klath."

The cart rolled forward, and we moved through the streets of Ostakis. As we did so, people came to the windows, and their doorways, and watched at the cart traveled the road.

I looked behind to see a group of people walking behind the cart, and more people joined as we rode the street. They wore determined and grim expressions on their faces. They carried clubs in their hands, and I feared they meant to harm me before I reached the church. But Mem was unconcerned.

Another group of young men joined, but these men were chanting.

"Free Aulkus! Down with Sharr!"

It was an uprising. The people of Ostakis were rallying around the House Klath or me. I did not know which.

Things would get ugly. But gave me hope for Ostakis that people took on danger to rid themselves of the pernicious influence of the Faith Progressive Church. But they were subjecting themselves to physical harm for the sake of their beliefs, and one never celebrates that.

Marta died because a religious fanatic took himself and several hundred people in his hypothetical next world.

I'd be damned if I let that happen again.

The Church Police did a better job this time of clearing the road of penitents, and we traveled nearly unchallenged to the church. Or maybe the line of angry men behind me frightened those that might have impeded my journey.

The church loomed before me, and Mem clutched my arm.

"*Yonsu*, I have a truck ready should this go badly for you."

"Sorry?" I stared at the church while bringing up the memory of the layout of the church and the courtyard.

"For your House, *Yonsu*. I have cousins in the country that will keep them until things calm down. For their safety."

"You would do this?" I asked incredulously. This man owed me nothing.

"Yes, *Yonsu*. We must keep the young Klath alive, mustn't we?"

The inheritance of House Klath passed through Arlan.

"Yes. Go to Irdrana Vos and tell her what you propose. Do as she says."

"*Yonsu*?"

"Please allow me to defer to the person who knows House Klath best."

"Yes, *Yonsu*. I will do as you say."

"And give her this for safe keeping."

"Yonsu," he said with wide eyes. What I handed him was the authority of Ostakis.

"I'll only give up my authority to Aulkus, but I won't let this ring fall into Sharr's hands."

He nodded thoughtfully. The cart halted with a jerk at the steps of the church.

"I see the wisdom of this, *Yonsu*," he said as he put the ring in a pocket of his overwrap. "May fortune follow you."

Fate. Fortune. In all the world we revisited humans never gave up this concept. Apparently, a belief in such was one defining mark of humanity.

"Thank you, *Syad* Mem. And good fortune to your house."

Four church guards emerged through the crowd.

"You will come with us, Ambassador," said one.

"Yes," I replied. "I will."

Chapter Twenty

ARLAN

"Pib!" I cried frantically with worry as we fled to the sanctuary room. "We have to get Pib!"

"I'll get him, *Yonsa*," said Edemar. "You sit and rest."

Thoughtfully, Pib brought work with him. He spread the ledgers before us and we sat and worked on the books as if everything would be all right. Father would return, and Kaj would come home and settle in with me to wait for the birth of our child.

But in the deepest part of my heart, I feared Sharr had gone too far, and two men would die this day. It had to be two because two was the number of balance.

I thought of numbers and the ancient wisdom attached to them. Nowadays we ignore the ancient meanings and look at numbers as the dry things we want them to be. But Ija was right, and I should not have dismissed her wisdom. That the Human Planets Collective sent only one man was unfortunate. They sought imbalance to test us. To restore the balance of Ostakis two men had to die. Which two out of Sharr, Kaj, or my father? My heart grew heavy considering the possibilities.

My eyes misted and I wiped away the offending wetness. Two out of three were bad odds, and I risked losing at least one man I loved most in the world, if not both.

Pib put his arm around me and put my head on his shoulder. "I wish we knew what was happening."

"Do you want to?" asked Ija.

"What do you mean, *ransee yinsee*?"

"Oh, you didn't," groaned Edemar.

"And what is it to you?" she said sharply.

"Do you have to bring that man in every room you inhabit?"

"What? Ija? Did you bring your holoscreen?"

"Of course the woman did," said Edemar in exasperation. "And I told her not to show it. I do not want you upset, *Yonsa*."

"I don't see how we can avoid that. Turn it on, Ija."

Ija pulled the black box out of a pocket from her overwrap and switched the machine on. It sputtered and spewed a static noise, and I worried it would not work inside this room. But she smacked the thing with her hand and the loathsome face of Reverend Sharr sprang up before us.

The focus of the holo was narrow, showing Sharr in High Holy Robes of black wrought with gold designs. As he spoke, the camera panned tightly to Kaj's face. My beloved stared at Sharr with a hard expression and his jaw set. Something terrible was about to happen. I clutched my hand to my chest as my heart sped. The camera focused on Sharr again.

"We have before us the unbeliever Kaj Deder, Earth Ambassador. He had sinned in the house of the sinner Aulkus Klath. He took the Cursed son of Klath to his bed, and he is unrepentant."

The camera whipped back to show my Kaj standing defiantly at the Shaming Post. This time a wider view panned, and I gasped. My father, arms, and legs locked in the post, did not move, and blood ran down his face. From the blood on Sharr's whip, it was clear he had whipped my father.

In public.

Thyenn Sharr killed the Trademaster of Ostakis for all to see.

I had only one comfort. Sharr did not have my father's large ring on his hand. Since he'd gone to outrageous lengths to claim it, I could only assume that Kaj put it somewhere safe.

But my father was dead, and it was horrible to see him, his eyes shut and bloody. I imagined his pain as Sharr laid the whip onto his body.

This time I could not wipe offending tears from my eyes. They came too quickly.

"The bastard," muttered Edemar.

Ija cupped her hands together and whispered a prayer of supplication, rocking in distress. Poor Ija never conceived Sharr was a cruel man, and now her image of her spiritual leader lay shredded along with the flesh of my father's back.

"Look," said Pib to me.

I ran my arm across my teary eyes and stared at the holo. Two guards stepped forward and unlocked my father and cast his body to the side.

Ija cried out as tears streamed from her eyes. "My Lord, my Lord, forgive the iniquities of this day." Her pained voice joined with my tears. Her grief keened with mine. My father was dead. How could I bear it?

"Now, Kaj Deder, you will repent for your sins," said Sharr.

The two guards took hold of Kaj's arms, but he gave each a cold glance. In one swift move, he fell backward and pulled them off balance. Then in a movement I'd never seen, he hopped forward seeming from the soles of his feet. He swung one guard into the other. The men stumbled against each other, and that was when he made his move.

He flew at Sharr and wrapped his arms around the man, one hand holding his chin, the other behind Sharr's head.

"You murdered my father-in-law," he declared. He didn't need to yell. The acoustics of the square magnified his voice.

Sharr struggled under him, but Kaj was bigger, and rage lit his eyes. I did not doubt he intended to kill Most Reverend Thyenn Sharr right there.

The crowd stood staring, but another set of voices filled the courtyard. Men in everyday dress poured in from all entrances screaming, "Death to Sharr! Down with the Church!" Some brandished torches, others sticks, and rocks. Others held bottles with rags in them, and I did not understand their purpose. The men with rocks threw them into the church windows, and enough of them hit the windows with such force that the beautiful painted glass cracked and shattered.

Then I saw the men with bottles, who held the rag-filled ends to the torches and threw them through the broken windows.

Several of the men jumped on the courtyard dais and pulled Sharr from Kaj's arms. He stepped backward, and then the world exploded.

"Kaj!" I screamed.

But the holoscreen blanked and filled with static.

We sat stunned. Tears ran down Ija's face. Edemar muttered obscenities, and Pib held me tight as I cried inconsolably.

The sanctuary door cracked open, and we looked up at Irdrana, who framed the doorway.

"Thank goodness. We have to go. Now. Hurry. There is a crowd of enraged people coming to this house, and I have to get you out of here."

"Irdrana?" I said.

"No time for questions. Quick."

We all stood and followed Irdrana out the back door and through the garden to the furthest end of it where a little-used service road ran. Along the way we collected Tolen who was working in the garden unconcerned or unknowing of the day's events. At the furthest reach of my father's property, a locked gate sat in the wood plank fence. Tolen opened the lock with his key from his key chain.

A delivery truck rattled down the dirt road at breakneck speed then pulled up short.

Serren Mem sat at the wheel and grinned. "Anyone looking for a ride?"

"What took you so long?"

"My cousin who owns this truck was not at home, which makes sense since he always talked about a day like this. I'm sure he was at the church. So I had to start the truck by unconventional means. Hurry, now. If it stalls, I may not be able to start it again."

We climbed into the back of the truck, which was empty but for large pads the size of blankets. But Tolen would not go with us.

"I'll go stay with my cousins," he said. "They will keep me safe."

"Good fortune to you, Tolen. I will see you soon."

"Yes, *Yonsa*, most assuredly."

Mem smiled and shut the door. "I have a cousin who lives on a farm outside the town. I will take you there."

The door shut, and we were in the dark.

THE ROCKING OF the truck on the rural rutted roads lulled me into an uneasy sleep. Exhaustion seeped from my bones as the child inside me took hold.

I dreamed Kaj was holding me and telling me not to worry. It was such a good dream I protested with a groan when a jolt woke me from it.

But a trill erupted in the dark, and I woke in alarm. Pib held me tightly and nuzzled my shoulder.

"Pib?"

"Arlan," he said miserably.

"What?" asked Irdrana in the dark. "Is he...?"

"Yes," I said.

Ija muttered prayers, and Edemar cursed. What a pair Ija and Edemar made. Pib was coming into his heat, and there was nothing for it.

"Are you okay, Edemar?" I asked.

"I am an old man," said Edemar. "The charms of a *syad* affect me not. I'll be fine."

"You sure?"

"Oh, yes," said Ija stopping her prayers. "I should know."

"Shut up, woman," said Edemar crossly.

Pib trilled again, and I gripped him. There was nothing I could do for him here because only a *yonsu* could relieve Pib of his heat.

But he was untried and yet the same age as I, which is probably why his parents arranged a partnership for him in Kiji Amst.

"Arlan," he keened, and his back arched.

I knew that suffering, that agony, of needing something so badly that it speared physical pain in his body.

The truck lurched to a stop. Irdrana scrambled past us and banged on the wall.

"Keep going," she yelled.

"Maybe we are at our destination?" asked Ija hopefully.

"No," she said. "We haven't traveled long enough."

The back of the truck opened, and the light from the sun blinded us. I heard footsteps land on the truck bed, and my heart sped in my chest. Had the Church police followed and finally caught up?

But when my eyesight cleared, I saw a nearly naked man standing over us, blocking the sun. But the shape was wrong. Rounder and squatter, he was not human, and I gasped in disbelief. He was an aboriginal, one of the race the colonists found when they landed here, the ones we called the Unspoken. We thought they were extinct.

Apparently, we were wrong.

And I caught the scent rolling off him.

Male. Definitely. My primal brain inspected his attributes and found him strong, lithe, commanding.

Pib's eyes fixed on him.

"*Syad*," said the man.

"Yes," said Pib.

The wild man pointed to himself. "*Yonsu.*"

"Yes," said Pib, as if the man answered a prayer.

The aboriginal sniffed at me. "*Syad.*"

I swallowed hard.

The man turned his head and rattled off words that I did not understand. Another of the strange men entered the cab, and the first one pointed to me.

But the second man went to Pib, and the first pushed him away. "Mine," he said.

My breath stuck in my throat, and my brain railed at this absurd turn of events. The second man pushed forward and picked me up.

"No!" I said.

But the second man laughed, and the first one rattled some harsh words at him.

"Sorry, little *syad*." He spoke in such a heavily accented Ostakian I could barely make out the words.

The first man picked up Pib and sprinted forward and jumped out of the truck.

"No," cried Ija.

Irdrana tried to grab the leg of the first man to hold him back, but he just kicked her and sent her flying to the back of the truck. Ija screamed.

"Mine," the second man said as he clutched me. The Unspoken pushed forward with every muscle bunched like a coiled spring and sailed out of the truck without effort.

I scanned what I could and saw the truck driver leaning out of the window of the cab. Whether he was unconscious or dead, I didn't know. But the Unspoken who held me ran after his fellows. I had to cling tightly against his loping stride as we ran across several fields and then a plain. He did not seem to tire as the miles stretched under us. Eventually we came to the shield wall our ancestors built against the desert. But it was in serious disrepair and parts fell in jagged heaps. The desert sands spilled through the opening as a bridge into the unforgiving land beyond.

The sun sank in the sky as our kidnappers hurried their pace onto the white sand filling the gaps in the wall. All I could do was hold on as my captor bore me away from all I knew.

Chapter Twenty-One

KAJ

The world exploded, and the concussive force slammed me to the ground. Fire ran through every bone as my ass and back met part of the church wall. Reflexively I covered my eyes with my arms. Flying glass stung my skin.

Putrid chemical smoke and green fire poured through the broken windows. Everywhere was chaos as penitents and protestors screamed. They pressed toward the entrances in great masses, achieving nothing but making it more possible for them to die.

A black cloud filled the courtyard, and I coughed and gagged. Jumping to my feet, I looked for another way to get out of this hell.

That's when I saw Thyenn Sharr.

His body lay broken against the church wall, his eyes glassy and his neck hanging limply to the side. It was what I intended to do for him before the protesters took him from me. I guess the Universe finished what I failed to do.

My eyes, nose, and mouth filled with tendrils of the black cloud pouring from one window. If I could not find a way out of here, away from the smoke, it would kill me.

I took my chances and jumped through a broken window, catching my foot on the sill, to propel me past the flames licking at the edges. I landed in a room familiar to me, the Holy Court of Thyenn Sharr. A drape behind Sharr's bench crawled with flames, and the air crackled and seared my skin. I ran for the front door, but I found the metal handle impossibly hot to the touch. I turned and sprinted to the back of the room, where the door to the inner chambers broke easily as I kicked it in.

And then I remembered that this was the door that Sharr brought prisoners through. Who knows how many people he had trapped behind bars while the fires raged about them?

I flew down the hall, not sure where I was going. A doorway to the left exuded the sour stench of urine and feces, the smells ascribed to human misery. I found that den of horrors where Sharr imprisoned his victims.

There was no lighting, and I stumbled several times on the stone stairs leading to the bottom. But it was a short stair, and when I stood, I could reach up and feel the ceiling.

At the top of the stair, the flames flared and hissed, sending an eerie light into the darkness. So I could not return that way.

I stumbled forward, and my left foot fell into something wet.

Wet and foul smells curled around my feet and the light from the stair revealed a channel cut in the floor where the effluence of the building flowed. It was a horrible hope that I found the sewer of this place. While it stank and was probably most unwholesome, it had to flow to somewhere outside this building.

I followed the channel as I moved through the undersides of this beast and it cut to the left. That was when I heard the sounds of human misery, moans, and cries. A light flared ahead, and I made for it. It was a goddamned pitch torch stuck in a holder in the wall, as if this place needed any more fire. There also was a huge ring of keys. I grabbed both and after fumbling a few more feet found the prisoner's cells.

"The church is burning," I said as I unlocked each lock. "We have to go."

I did not look at the men there because there was no time to assess each one. Wood beams, the bones on which the church rested, groaned, and we all had to move before they caved in and buried us in our final grave.

A small crowd gathered behind me, and I led them forward toward the channel's end. I had no idea what would greet us when we reached the end or if there was a way we could escape.

The ceiling abruptly ended in a spectacular vault that soared above us in a dome with a skylight. The channel poured, as I feared, out of a hole too small for anyone to escape through. In fact, effluence gathered here, unable to clear the small hole and stank more than the cells.

"*Yonsu, Yonsu!*" chattered one unfortunate. "There!"

I looked toward where he pointed across the channel to a door.

A door.

I stared at the jangling metal in my hands and disbelieved I might hold the key to my freedom. One man pulled the ring from my hands and tried each key frantically to find the one that fit the lock.

"*Yonsu!*" Another man pointed to the wall on our right through where the flame blazed between chinks in the walls. Where we entered, the wood in the beams screamed and crashed into the hall as the building dissolved in heat and fire.

Finally, my compatriot found the key. The door swung open, and he cried out, "*Yonsu*, come here!"

I pushed forward and found the water came to the door's ledge, stinking of human waste. But there was nothing for it. Either we swam through the shit to gain our freedom, or we died here.

"Go," I said, urging each man forward. And none complained. One by one each man fell into the water and swam, or dog-paddled toward the water's edge.

One man floundered, however, and screamed for help. I jumped and used the skills learned in some long-ago water class. I got under him and pulled his chin up out of the fetid water. He thrashed at first, then stilled when he realized I would hold him up. With that, I crawled with my free hand and kicked our way to shore. When we got to shallow enough water, he scrambled to shore.

The prisoners stood at the edge of the water. A firehose wielded by stout men that drew water out of a firetruck showered the men with clean water and beyond them stood two men with sheets. One by one, the men peeled away their reeking clothing. After the fire crew doused them clean, others wrapped the shivering men in the sheets. Men in civil police uniforms spoke with the rescued occupants of Sharr's den of hell.

I stood there, waiting for my turn under the hose, when a familiar face emerged from the crowd held back beyond the fire truck.

Mar Seyatt looked me up and down and grinned. "I always knew you'd end up covered in shit. I guess I was right."

AN HOUR LATER, I sat in Mar Seyatt's office in his robe, sipping tea, while we waited for Silar to bring me fresh clothes. Seyatt had a convenient shower there, since his workspace was more like a small apartment than a place of governmental business. But I soon gathered that Mar Seyatt, despite his jovial nature, hardly stopped working, and probably lived here.

One man after another came into the office and offered their reports of what happened in the city. It was grim. People continued to riot in the streets and the hospital overfilled to capacity. They triaged the injured in the hospital courtyard, and more people waited at the gates.

The fire in the church still burned but Seyatt long ago gave the order to let it. The Kiji Ost Fire Brigade didn't have the correct equipment to save such a large structure. The city police, the Church police, and the firefighters joined forces to break up the riots. Firefighters sprayed water trying to disperse the crowds. The joined police forces set up perimeters in different sections to contain groups of people so the fighting wouldn't spread.

Worry etched lines in Seyatt's face as one report after another came in. I felt for him. The city services didn't have the resources to deal with this extreme level of violence. But soon word came in about fighting in Dastoan Heights, and I worried about Arlan and the household.

"It will settle down after nightfall," said Seyatt.

"Why? Violence often joins the same in the dark."

"Yes. But I've ordered the city lights off tonight. People will have no way to see in the dark."

It sounded like something that Sharr would say, and I shuddered when I remembered the lifeless eyes of the head of the Faith Progressive Church.

Yes. My job was assassin, but I was untried in my trade. When it came down to it, I couldn't squeeze the life out of Thyenn Sharr. I was glad those men took him. I was sorry they died when he did. They died because I failed.

Another knock on the door and two men entered. Silar held a bundle of clothing. The other was Serren Mem.

"*Yonsu* Seyatt, *Yonsu* Klath," he said as he bowed. "I am sorry to report a terrible thing."

"What?" Seyatt asked tiredly in a day of horrible things.

"I sent the House Klath members out of the city as *Yonsu* Klath instructed, but the truck stopped on the road, and the two Cursed were taken."

I sat straighter in my chair and put the tea on Seyatt's desk. "Who took who?"

"We don't know," said Mem.

"I know," said Irdrana at the door. Two of Seyatt's men held her back as if she had nothing important to say.

"Let her in," said Seyatt irritably. "Sorry, Irdrana."

Irdrana, tired and streaked with dirt, stood before us with her eyes filled with fire. "Two Unspoken ambushed the truck and took Pib and Arlan."

"Arlan?" I asked.

Seyatt pursed his lips. "Unspoken? Are you sure?"

Irdrana put her hands on her hips. "Why do you question me, Mar Seyatt? I saw with my own eyes what they were. And they were not human."

"Not human?" I asked. "What do you mean?"

"The original people of this planet," sighed Seyatt.

"Are you telling me there is an indigenous people on this planet?"

He gave a grim nod. "There were many when the settlers came. And we used them for labor and other things. But as they assimilated into our society, they died out as a people. Or so we thought."

Seyatt said the words so easily, and yet they struck me as strongly as thunderbolts. "You used indigenous people? A nonhuman species? Subsumed into your society? And you did not think that violated your charter?"

"Do not judge us, Kaj," said Seyatt. "Earth was far away, and the settlers found Ostakis was not the paradise promised. Half of them died in the first year. If we did not incorporate the indigenous people, our colony would have died."

My breath hitched in my shock. We suspected something happened to the human genome, but we thought it might have been a mutation or a series of such. And what we would have given to find another species other than our own. We settled hundreds of worlds and had yet to discover living sentient beings that evolved on their own planet.

We had thought we were alone.

And we weren't.

And now they had Arlan.

"We have to find Arlan." I said.

"How?" said Seyatt. "The city is in shambles. I have no men to spare."

Chapter Twenty-Two

ARLAN

Night fell, and the air chilled. The moon rose high and full and cast enough light where I could see the ground below. I shivered as my muscles and bones ached from my kidnapper holding me in one position too long.

My captor's companion turned right after we hiked the sand bridge. We followed the wall on which the moon's light fell, revealing dark cracks and fissures in the once smooth wall. He trilled a sound into the night, and we slowed and then stopped. My sandals sank into the sand, which was still warm from the relentless daytime sun.

Pib, ahead of me, though his captor put him down, clung to the man, who stroked Pib's hair and neck gently. Pib's bun had fallen apart, and his light brown hair fell about his shoulders. The aboriginal seemed fascinated with it.

One by one, others emerged from cracks within the thick wall until ten gathered around us. Their broad faces smiled as they poked us with their fingers and jabbed at our captors, making playful noises. The two put up with this patiently for a short time and then Pib's captor waved them away, speaking too fast in their language for me to understand.

But I recognized some of the sounds as they were in part our language. Now I understood why the homeworld language was so different from ours. We had spliced the aboriginal language into it. Ostakian was a mix of the old world and the new.

Pib trilled, and the aboriginal responded by pulling him closer. I was horrified, but Pib was not. He smiled at the man and rubbed his face on the man's shoulder.

I was horrified at what would happen tonight. Frantically, I ran from the man who carried me all this way, and vainly threw myself between Pib and the aboriginal.

But my captor pulled me back and dragged me into the seam of rock.

The aboriginals, it seemed, had been busy. They had carved tunnels from the cracks within the construction and broke and rearranged rock in familiar motifs that buttressed openings and walkways. I realized the patterns were much like the mosaics in my father's office building.

The stonework arrangements made utter sense speaking in an ancient heuristic that said, "This goes here, and that goes there." But it was architecturally sound. For the first time, I understood the way I had been looking at numbers also governed how I constructed the patterns of my thinking.

And apparently that of the aboriginals.

My captor pulled me into a chamber lit with a soft glow. Light came from sconces carved into the stone, and inside I saw oval cullen eggs glowing from within. How did this happen? I did not know cullen were bioluminescent.

His fellow entered the chamber with Pib, who was stroking the man's body shamelessly.

"Pib?" I asked.

But he did not answer me. His glazed eyes stared at his captor. The two entered another chamber, one where I saw something like bedding spread on the floor. A covering dropped and veiled the entrance.

I would be sick.

My captor pulled me to another chamber, and I struggled, but he just laughed. He pointed to a pile of bedding, and I shook my head. Surely he understood that universal gesture.

He smiled too broadly.

"No worry," he drawled, or close enough that I understood that much of what he said. "Sit. We traveled a long time."

I was exhausted, so I did. He riffled through baskets by the wall and brought out bowls and a leather bladder.

"Eat," he said. "Baby needs food."

It stunned me that he knew I was pregnant.

He dropped next to me and pulled what looked like jerky from one bowl and offered it to me. "Eat."

I did not know what it was, but I had to assume it was edible. It kept him alive and it should me too. I bit into it tentatively. Though chewier than I was used to, the smoked meat tasted flat. I had to wonder how old this jerky was, or from what animal the flesh came.

He pointed to himself. "Jhono."

So we were exchanging names now. I pointed to my chest. "Arlan."

He snorted as if he found my name funny.

"Yeah," I said indignantly. "Jhono? What's Jhono?"

He took the hint and sobered. Then he gazed at me fiercely. "Jhono *yonsu*."

Obviously, Jhono had some experience talking with humans, because I heard his fellow speak in complete sentences to their tribe. No. Jhono wanted me to understand him and carefully picked out our shared words to accomplish that.

"You may be," I replied crisply. "But you are not my *yonsu*."

He understood half the sentence at least. No, my and *yonsu* were words shared in our different languages. He frowned.

He pointed to me then him. "Mine."

I scoffed. "Don't think so."

He made a little shrug of his shoulders as if what I said was of no consequence.

"You will like me," he said confidently. Then he leered, "Mating."

I shivered again, and he pulled me close.

"Cold?" he asked in a concerned voice.

"Frightened," I said.

"No fear, *syad*. No hurry. Not like them."

He jerked his thumb toward the chamber where Pib and the other male lay. I tried to shut out their mating cries, but they were getting very loud. He laughed, and then incredulously Jhono rubbed my stomach.

"Small baby." He smiled and kissed my head. "Lucky," he said. "Don't work hard like Acho for his."

Aside from the fact that Jhono was a kidnapper, he was affable. I saw if all aboriginals were like him why humans would find them easy to exploit.

"Sleep?" he said.

The word he used translated into "lie with" which could convey as sleep or sex and I was not sure what he meant. I wanted to head off any notion of the latter.

"No," I said firmly.

"Baby needs sleep," he said.

I jerked my thumb to Acho and Pib's chamber. "Loud."

Jhono rumbled, stroked my hair and trilled.

"Future," he said.

"No," I said. I couldn't conceive of being with anyone but Kaj, who I saw blown apart on Ija's holoscreen. And I couldn't hold it in anymore. Remembering the sight of my father's dead body and the explosion that blotted out Kaj destroyed me. Tears flowed freely in my grief.

"*Syad?*" Jhono looked on me with concern. My kidnapper clutched me and drew my head to his chest and rocked as if to soothe an upset child. He trilled softly, a sound that was almost a song.

Next door Pib and Acho's mating sounds came to a fever pitch, and they were both screaming. I tensed. What did this mean for Pib? Did the aboriginal claim him or merely had sex with him? And with Pib in heat, what kind of child would he bear if he got pregnant?

"Ssh, ssh, little *syad*," said Jhono, still rocking me. "They like it. You will like it future time after the baby."

I tried to pull away. "No. I will not."

He touched my face, and I turned my head away. But that movement must have shifted the fabric because he pulled aside my underwrap and touched Kaj's mating mark. Jhono sniffed at it.

"Where *yonsu?*" he asked.

My *yonsu?* Kaj? Tears fell again.

"Bad *yonsu*," he scolded.

"No. Not his fault."

"Bad *yonsu*. *Syad* cry. No good. No good."

I bit my lip hard, willing away the tears. As much as I wanted to spend my grief, I would not do it in the arms of my kidnapper.

"You sleep, *syad*. Baby needs sleep."

He pulled me down with him and wrapped his body around mine, stroking my hair.

"Pretty," he trilled. "Pretty *syad* makes pretty babies," he said.

I lay on the pallet of my kidnapper, and he dropped off and lightly snored in my ear. So, as he said, he wouldn't force himself on me. Just kidnap me and take me far away from anyone I knew.

But he's a good guy, really.

I snorted at my own sad joke as Pib and Acho in the next room continued with the wild sounds of their passion.

Chapter Twenty-Three

KAJ

Seyatt ordered guards to escort Irdrana home. But before she left, she hugged me and pressed a hard object in my hand.

"Take care, Trademaster," she whispered in my ear.

She pulled away and left quickly. I looked at my hand to find the ring of House Klath. With a sigh, I put it on my finger, remembering when Arlan did so. He did not realize the finger he slid it on was the traditional one where I once wore a wedding ring. But it touched me when he did so.

Seyatt and I were alone in the office aside from the messengers and mayoral assistants, who made a steady procession in and out of Seyatt's office. Night fell quickly and as Seyatt promised the city lights did not shine. If people were walking about, they were doing so with personal lamps that made them subject to detainment if caught. The combined police forces walked the streets trying to enforce Seyatt's curfew.

"*Yonsu* mayor," said one of Seyatt's assistants as he rushed in. "Our spaceport received a message from the homeworld ship."

"So," said Seyatt. "I won another bet."

"Bet?"

"With Aulkus. He said the ship left. I said it did not. Are you going to pay up for House Klath?"

"We'll discuss this bet when this is over. I want details of this betting you did on me."

"*Yonsu* mayor?"

"Yes, yes," said Seyatt with annoyance.

"The homeworld ship inquired into the fate of Kaj Deder."

Seyatt shot me a pointed look. "And should I take this to mean that they are listening to our transmissions?"

"Perhaps they found Sharr's sermons interesting."

"Tell them he is alive and well."

"No," I said. "Don't tell them that."

"Why?"

"I do not want them to know I'm alive."

Seyatt grunted and looked at me with suspicion. "And what should I tell them?"

"Tell them insurgents captured me."

Seyatt put his hand on his chin and nodded. "Okay, we will do that." He still regarded me with suspicion. "House Klath has supported me for many years so I will honor your request. I do expect a full explanation when things are more settled."

"Of course, *Yonsu* Mayor."

I worried about Arlan and our child that he carried. I found it difficult to sit when he was in danger while someone brought me tea.

But I must wait for events to unfold, and while I did, I went into Seyatt's bathroom and dressed in the clothes Silar brought. They weren't light, or comfortable, and I wished I had Ostakian wraps.

Another messenger arrived, and he wore the messenger service colors of Serren Mem. I had learned many things that day, and one of them was that each of the messenger services wore a particular color.

I came out, and another of Serren Mem's messengers arrived.

"*Yonsu* Mayor, my sources tell me that a homeworld ship is flying toward the barrier wall."

"Thank you," said Seyatt. "You may leave."

"Excuse me," I said. "When the HPC ship lands, I will need the coordinates. Can you get me that?"

The messenger looked to Seyatt who gave him a nod.

"Yes, *Yonsu*."

"Very good. And ask Serren Mem if I can get transportation to or close to that location."

"Yes, *Yonsu*. I will return shortly."

"Humph," said Seyatt. "You are using your people to find Arlan, aren't you? How did you accomplish that?"

"My HPC pin. You remember it. It is a locator beacon."

"I see," said Seyatt.

"I gave it to Arlan as a precaution. You do understand that my people would not do this on my request. Since my mission is complete, they want to know if I live. If I do, they expect me to return to them to deploy to the next assignment."

"Your mission?"

"To neutralize Thyenn Sharr."

"You don't intend to return to them, do you?" asked Seyatt.

Did I? If this whole sad affair taught me anything, I was unsuited for the task for which I trained. Seeing Aulkus dead, and Sharr's body smashed to pieces, I no longer had the desire to deal death. Or seek it. The anger and pain in my heart over Marta's death dissolved to a whisper of regret for what might have been. And Arlan. He bore my child. In my heart, I was sure of it, and I could not abandon him. And I did not want to.

"No, I don't intend to go back to the HPC ship," I said hoarsely. If the thought rolled around in my head before this, it was ephemeral and more like a wish. Speaking the words gave them form and purpose.

Seyatt nodded his head.

"I misjudged you, Kaj, and I'm sorry. It seemed the homeworld would send a man whose only concerns were for economic conquest, and cultural assimilation. I did not understand what Aulkus and Irdrana saw in you."

"You weren't far wrong. I was the tool of the HPC's agenda."

Another messenger rushed in.

"*Yonsu* Klath, as requested, your transport waits downstairs."

"We'll talk about that agenda later," said Seyatt. "I sincerely hope that you find Arlan safe and well."

I held out my hand to Seyatt. "Thank you, Mar. I hope as Aulkus did, I can count you as a friend."

He gave me an effusive smile and clasped my forearm.

"I like you better now that you are Kaj Klath. It sounds better than Deder."

SERREN MEM SMILED at me when I climbed into the cart.

"I go with you, *Yonsu*, to make sure you don't come to harm."

"My house is honored by your service," I replied, though it confused me why he personally drove the cart.

"No. No service. It was my fault you lost your *yonsa*. I should not have stopped on the road."

"What happened?"

"I saw a body on the road and stopped. They attacked."

"So they tricked you."

"Yes, *Yonsu*. But it is no secret it is dangerous driving in those parts."

"My house does not hold your house to blame," I said.

"My house appreciates your generosity."

The cart lurched forward and traveled the eerily quiet streets. Seyatt's curfew seemed to hold fast, as we were the only people on the street except for police who stood around fires lit in metal barrels. I think again of the meaning about Mem's words about the danger of those roads.

"From what you say, *Syad* Mem, the Unspoken are not strangers in those parts."

Mem frowned. "We do not speak of this."

"Meaning, if the authorities knew, there would be punishments."

Mem shrugged. "Not so much that. There are those of us who honor the ancient people. If Sharr knew of them, he'd hunt them."

"Sharr is not a problem anymore."

"But the Church is not a building or just one man," said Mem. "It is the people who go to it. Sharr and his kind spent hundreds of years building walls of hate between the old ones and us. People raised with such ideas don't discard them easily. We cut off the head of the beast, but the body lives."

I saw the wisdom in Mem's words. Cultural change is slow. We took hundreds of years to erase the religious excesses of the Theocracy, and even with that pockets of hold-outs remained.

"So whatever happens, you want me to keep secret my knowledge of the old ones."

"I do not presume to tell a *yonsu* what he should do. But I find that idea agreeable."

"I will not talk about the Old Ones with the people of Ostakis. But I may report this to the HPC. This is important information, one that affects what decisions the HPC makes regarding this planet."

"I understand, *Yonsu*."

We reached the outer limits of the city, and a box truck waited for us at the end of the paved road. Mem beckoned me to the cab of the vehicle. I sat in the seat next to the driver while Mem took a position on a bench behind the cab seats. He spoke in rapid Ostakian to the driver, who grunted and started the truck. So we continued into the short-lived night to the edges of dawn. Finally, the truck cut to a sharp right, and we drove toward the enormous shield wall over a heavily rutted road. When the wall loomed over us well into the sky, the truck stopped.

"*Yonsu*, we must walk from here."

"How far?"

"A few miles. But there is no guarantee the first place we look is where we will find Arlan. The Old Ones often move to different warrens they have."

I dropped to the ground, and Mem gave stern instructions to the driver. The driver argued, and Mem said loudly, "Yes, yes, you will receive payment."

"Is there a problem?"

"My cousin, the Lord protect him, worries he will not get compensated."

I stuck my head inside the cabin.

"The Trademaster of Ostakis guarantees your payment," I said. The man glared at me, and I did not get a good feeling.

"*Syad*, tell him to come with us."

Mem nodded, and he spoke rapidly to his cousin who swore but got out of the truck.

"Let's go," I said. I tried to appear confident but inside my guts churned. I worried Arlan had come to harm. This spurred me on despite walking any length in this gravity pulled too much at my muscles and bones. I must get to him.

Mem took up the front position and the driver the last, and we walked single file to the wall. I missed the entrance, but Mem did not. He slipped in between a crevice, and I followed him into another world.

The wall was not solid as I supposed. Inside a slab, a paved pathway cut through. Along the walls, a soft glow emanated from sconces, giving us enough light to see. I was fascinated by them.

"What is this place?" I asked.

"Just a path to the other side. The old ones make their homes in the sandward side of the wall."

The wall was thick, but I saw where the entire construction was hollow and built on succeeding arches, so the walls honeycombed with tunnels. We came out on the other side just as the sun peeked over the horizon. It was bright and hurt my eyes, but I was not the only one who turned from it.

"Come," said Mem. He turned right and moved with certainty along the wall.

"What do you trade with them?" I asked.

"Who, *Yonsu*?"

"The original natives of Ostakis."

"I should not talk about these things with the Trademaster."

"Why?" I suspected such trade was illegal or at least skirted the law.

Mem glanced over his shoulder at me.

"The Old Ones are most proficient at producing raw cullen silk. I do not want my supply of that cloth taken over by the larger textile houses. They will not pay what the labor is worth."

"I note your altruism, *Syad* Mem."

"The Trademaster makes a joke at an inopportune time," said Mem.

"Sorry." My frayed nerves were showing.

"My house apologizes," said Mem. "You have suffered a great loss today and worry for your partner, while stupidly I talk business."

"My house apologizes as well. I have called upon your services one too many times this day."

"Mine is always at the service of House Klath. You have done us a great service this day."

Did I? I wondered what people said about what happened at the church. While I achieved the HPC objectives, now Ostakis had to live with the consequences of my actions.

It was something to sort out when things weren't so dire.

Mem stopped and trilled the sounds that I heard Arlan make while we occupied the sanctuary room. I froze, not knowing what this meant. But another trill answered.

"They come, Trademaster," said Mem. And he dropped to the sand waiting for the Old Ones, and I did the same.

Chapter Twenty-Four

ARLAN

A trill rang through the chambers of the Unspoken's cave, and Jhono stirred next to me. He rose from the pallet, muttering, and stepped over me to exit the room. Acho joined him. Whatever was happening was important enough for him to rise from his mating bed.

Pib stumbled from Acho's chamber. I threw my arms around his body as much to reassure myself as to steady him.

"Are you okay?" I asked.

He smiled at me broadly, his eyes hazy, and he sighed. "Yes. I am fine."

I stared at several mating bites on Pib's neck. "You sure? He looks like he was rough with you."

"Honestly, I didn't notice. It was all fire and needs, and wonderful."

"But Pib, he's, he's—" I failed in my words because what I wanted to say sounded wrong to my head.

It did to Pib too. "What? An Unspoken? So what? We are as much a part of them as we are humans like Kaj. In fact, we are much more like the Unspoken than the homeworlders. Acho told me that everyone is like us, Cursed, though they don't call it that, and switch roles when the heats come."

"What? You understood what he said?"

"He took his time and yes, the meanings were clear. We share a lot of language with them."

"I noticed. But the Unspoken said he was a *yonsu*."

"Their idea of *yonsu* is not ours, Arlan. A *yonsu* is a hunter, protector or seeking a mate. And *syad* is a person in heat or pregnant. It's not a status defining role."

"With all that going on last night, you had time for these discussions?"

Pib's face colored, but then he smirked. "We didn't sleep at all. And we took breaks."

Acho turned. "*Syad*, I go. You stay."

"Go?" Pib frowned.

"Business. You rest."

"Are we together or not?" asked Pib with a stern expression on his face.

"*Syad*," said Acho gently. "One time you stay. I go. Will return soon."

Acho snapped his finger to the crowd forming at the door of the chamber.

"Food for *syads*," he commanded. Some of those gathered rushed off.

Jhono turned and stroked my cheek. "Return soon, pretty *syad*."

He followed Acho out of the chamber, and several Unspoken followed carrying baskets.

"You seem to get along pretty well with yours," smirked Pib.

"Don't even joke about it. I can't even think in that direction since—"

I couldn't say it since Kaj died. Tears formed in my eyes, and Pib hugged me.

"I'm sorry," he said. "Or course. I was a jerk. Forgive me."

He held me for which I was grateful. But I also noticed a lack of noise in the cave. I poked my head from the chamber and saw no one else.

"Come on," I said. My sandals crunched on the sand as I stepped forward but I did not hear Pib's. I glanced over my shoulder to find Pib frozen in his spot.

"We're leaving."

He shook his head. "No. I don't want to go."

"Why not?"

Pib balled his fists and swallowed hard. "Because I like it here. I fit. And to what do I have to return?"

I stared at him in surprise. For the first time in his life, Pib stood up for what he wanted. But this can't be his life. It's too wild and uncertain. Pib living among the aboriginals? No.

"House Klath."

Pib scoffed. "And what? Wait until my parents sell me off again? Or send me to Shaming once more?"

A small noise stuck in my throat. He was right, but how could I let him go?

"I won't let that happen."

"How can you stop it? They have the legal rights, not you. Or me. They can disown me a thousand times and claim me just as many." His voice was bitter, and I did not blame him. Pib gazed at me with a plea in his eyes.

"You'll be happy here?"

He nodded. "Yes."

"If that is what you want."

"Stay."

My heart ached at this request. I did not want to lose my best friend, but as my eyes swept the cave I knew it, and Jhono were not my life.

I shook my head. "No, Pib. I have no desire for that. I want my child raised in House Klath. Irdrana and Seyatt will help me. I'm sure."

"Your guy there will be mighty disappointed," he said jerking his finger towards Jhono's bedchamber.

I shrugged my shoulders. "Tell him I'm sorry. I just wanted to go home."

Pib threw his arms around me, knocking me back a step. "I'm going to miss you, Arlan. You are the best friend a man could ever have."

I held on longer than I should. Time ticked and the Unspoken could return any minute, especially the ones who would bring us food.

"I love you, Pib Alluven. You are the brother I never had."

"Get out of here," he said hoarsely. "Or I won't let you leave."

He pushed me, and I pulled away and stumbled toward the cave's entrance. The steps to the portal seemed to take forever, and my heart thundered in my chest because I was afraid one of the Unspoken would discover me. The entrance beckoned with the sun shining brightly through it. This close to the entrance, heat from the outside seeped in, and I baked in it.

With a final push, I propelled myself out the shelter of the wall and onto the blazing sand. Immediately I thought of returning and making my escape at night, but I did not know if I would get this opportunity again.

The sun sat a little above the horizon, so in that direction lay East. I needed to go West, but to do so, I had to find a sand bridge through a gap in the wall.

So North it was, and my feet slipped in the warm sand as I trod toward my goal. It tired me quickly. The sun beat relentlessly on me, I had no sleep the night before, and little food. I was woefully unprepared for the brutal task I set for myself.

My heart thudded in my chest as I grew thirstier. Within an hour I felt hot and lightheaded. I stopped a minute to catch my breath and swayed on my feet. I stumbled toward the wall on my left. At this time of day, there was no shadow, but I hoped to find a crevice in which to find shelter.

"Arlan!" I heard.

It sounded like Kaj's voice, which was not possible. Was I hallucinating?

"Arlan!" said another—Pib's voice.

This is bad. Dehydrated and hearing things, I sank against the wall finding no shelter there. Only heat.

And despair.

My father dead.

Kaj dead.

I was alone.

Perhaps this was better. My father and I didn't believe in Thyenn Sharr's heaven, one where the Lord of all gods embraced believers purified of sin. But perhaps a place existed where I could be with my father and Kaj again.

The sun was too hot. I slipped into the space between wakefulness and sleep. *I'll just die like this.*

That would be fine with me.

"Arlan!"

Rough hands shook me, and I woke with the sun in my eyes, so I saw nothing. Maybe I was still asleep.

Or dead.

"Water!" demanded the voice, the one so much like Kaj's.

A hand cradled my head as liquid splashed on my lips. The sensation snapped me to consciousness.

Ice-blue eyes gazed at me with concern. And his skin was pale though burned red by the sun.

"Arlan?" he asked again.

"Kaj!" I said. I threw my arms around him. My heart leaped with joy as I pressed my face to his shoulder. "Kaj! What? Why..."

"What were you thinking?" he scolded. "Why did you do this? Did you not know you'd die out here without water in this heat?"

I coughed, and he pushed me back and made me drink more water.

The liquid slid down my throat, and nothing had ever tasted so good. Finally, I pushed it away.

"I thought you were dead," I blurted.

"Well, it nearly killed me to find you weren't where Jhono said. I nearly had a heart attack. Don't do that to me again."

I met his eyes and saw more than concern for my welfare, more than worry. It was something I never thought I'd see from a man.

Love.

"On one condition, Kaj."

"What?"

"Take me home."

WE ARRIVED AT House Klath several hours later. I did not know how long, because I slept, between times when Kaj woke me and made me drink water again. He told me bits of his story before I fell asleep once more.

When we got home Edemar took a long time to answer the door, but the city police that Seyatt posted said members of House Klath were inside.

Finally, the door opened. Irdrana peered around the corner then pulled the door open with a yank.

Immediately she threw her arms around us. "Oh thank the Lord you are safe!"

We walked into a house in disarray. They had painted ugly words on the atrium's walls and scored the beautiful and rare dining set with nasty carvings. Delicate antique vases and sculpture lay smashed on the floor, and the paneled walls bore deep scratches.

"After Sharr died," said Irdrana, "people went crazy. A group of penitents attacked the house. I'm sorry. They destroyed the gardens too."

"Sharr's dead?" I asked stupidly.

"Yes," said Kaj.

"You didn't say. How?"

"I had his head in my arms, and all it would take was one twist—"

I breathed sharply, but Kaj continued.

"But the crowd pulled him away from me. And then one of the homemade bombs exploded and threw Sharr and me against the wall. When I came to, he was dead."

His eyes held a haunted look, and I suspected Kaj would carry the image of a dead Sharr with him always.

Just like I would carry the image of my father lying lifeless on the Shaming post.

We looked through the rest of the house and saw the damage.

Kaj clucked his tongue. "It looks like we have a lot of work to do here."

"We?" I asked.

"If you'll have me," he said.

Chapter Twenty-Five

KAJ

Dearest Marta,

It is time to say good-bye. Just as you foresaw, I found the young man with the golden shards in his eyes. He loves me with the fierceness of an Ostakian sandstorm, relentless and unabatingly, and my soul burns like the bright Ostakian sun for him. We have a good life, and a child, and more down the road if we want.

Of this, Arlan asked that if we should have a girl that we name her Marta. When I asked why, he said, "Because without her you would not have found me." It is some weird Ostakian logic that I will spend my life parsing. But in this, I think he means that you taught me what love was and that when I found Arlan, I could recognize it again.

I will always love you, Marta. Like Arlan, I thank you for teaching me what love is.

This time I watched from the bottom of the stairs instead of at the top of the landing. The new ambassador's skin was dark brown, and she wore a dashiki dress with a short skirt.

Interesting choice. How soon would it be until she adopted the Ostakian habit of covering most of her body?

We—Irdrana, Seyatt, Arlan and I—decided that for the sake of Ostakis, we would pretend what Earth wanted to believe. The first Earth Ambassador failed in his mission and caused a riot. Earth sent their profuse apologies and a ship of iron ore to redress the Earth Ambassador's crimes.

Oh, they anticipated crimes. They sent that ship only months after mine left Earth.

The second ambassador had a staff, and they crowded around her on the platform. She was the one who they intended to work to bring Ostakis into the Human Planet's Collective.

"They sent a woman," said Seyatt, frowning.

"I wouldn't take any meaning to that," I said. I wondered though if posting a woman was a subtle hint to Ostakis.

Probably.

"Why are her legs showing?" said Irdrana, perplexed.

"It is the fashion on Earth. If a woman chooses to, she can."

"Can we take that as a message?" Seyatt said.

"Mar, if you do not, you are a fool."

Seyatt snorted, long used to my dry humor. But he did not laugh because he also knew if he showed improper behavior now, I would keep the wine drinking to a respectable level. He liked my wine too much for that.

The ambassador's face beaded with sweat as she labored down the stairs, but she managed a grace I did not feel upon my arrival here.

Irdrana stepped forward and greeted the new ambassador. They exchanged ritual greetings. Irdrana made the introductions. The ambassador, Abena Kamali, stared at me too long, with questions in her eyes, but my appearance had changed in the past year. Ostakis suntanned me as dark as a native and bleached my blond hair white. I also lost two inches in height from living in Ostakis' heavier gravity. Arlan liked to tease me about how he lost his exotic off-world lover to the bright sun of Ostakis. My eyes were still blue, but there were rare blue-eyed Ostakians. And I wore the customary wraps Ostakians wore so I was indistinguishable from a native-born citizen. I was no offworlder now.

I invited them to daymeal, and Abena smiled, thinking this a great honor. In a way it was, but since Aulkus died, not so much.

I was no Aulkus Klath.

The driver, by my order, took us to the Dastoan Direct by way of Veller Point. It was no longer called Church Point. This was the long way around, but I wanted to show the ambassador where her offices would sit. Abena smiled charmingly as we traveled through the city, but when we passed the hulking remains of the Faith Progressive Church, she frowned.

The smoke had long since died, but when the wind blew, you still caught a whiff of charcoal.

"What happened there?" Abena asked.

"An act of terrorism, I'm afraid," I said.

"Oh," she said with dismay. "Will they rebuild?"

"Not in this city," I said sourly. *And not if I can help it.* After the uprising, the church elders thought it politic to relocate. We did not stop them.

"They have a cathedral far to the North in Kiji Amst," said Irdrana. That was where the church with their new Most High Reverend moved the Church's base of operations.

And good riddance to the Faith Regressive Church.

"Besides," I said. "We start demolition on it next month. We are building a new legate there for international trade and relations. Your office will be there, and I made sure it will have a beautiful view overlooking the lake. We will name it the Aulkus Klath Trade and International Relations Center."

"Named for?"

"Arlan's father. He gave his life to further the cause of trade between worlds. It was the least we could do to honor him."

We drove through the Garden District and arrived at the Ambassador's house. The driver stopped as pre-instructed. This would be a brief visit before we went to mine for daymeal. But this visit was more for Silar and the house staff, who were not accustomed to a woman as their *yonsu*. I had promised Silar I would make the introductions to ease the ambassador into the household.

"This is your house," said Irdrana, and the Ambassador's face crinkled in alarm. I could guess her thoughts. It was too big and too ostentatious. Irdrana, Seyatt and I got out, and I held my hand to the Ambassador to help her out of the cart.

"Mine?" she said, perplexed. "It is far too much."

"No, Madam Ambassador," said Irdrana. "It matches your new rank here. Your job is essential to Ostakis, and you'll need a house befitting your new station."

"Did the old ambassador live here?"

Irdrana shot me a glance, asking me to provide the correct response.

"I believe Kaj Deder spent one night here before all the disruptions started. Are you concerned of negative connotations of being associated with that?"

It was a stunningly honest and undiplomatic question, and Abena blushed.

"I just want to get off on the right foot."

"Pardon?" I said, acting as if I didn't understand her colloquial words, as any Ostakian wouldn't.

"Do not concern yourself, Madam Ambassador," said Irdrana. "Clerics have thoroughly cleansed it."

Irdrana tried to hide her mirth at her joke, but I saw her eyes glitter in amusement.

I shot Irdrana a sharp glance. At her urging, I told Irdrana the proper term of Earth address. I never thought she'd use it. Irdrana did not agree with my decision not to tell the Ambassador I was formerly Kaj Deder and dropped this hint. I shook my head, and she smiled. Always bucking the system, that one.

There was no need for me to hide. The HPC ship departed at the official notification of my "death." The people who sent us on this mission were long dead and forgotten in all but the records of the diplomatic corp. Those who would read Abena's report hadn't been born.

We went to the house, and Silar opened the door. He spoke the ritual words, and Abena said her part. Silar presented the house staff, and Abena thanked them for their service.

Silar gave me a concerned look, but I just smiled reassuringly.

"We will bring back your *yonsu* after daymeal."

Irdrana, Seyatt, and I had decided we would insist that all will address Abena as *yonsu*, not the lesser form of *yonsa*. She would have the full authority of a *yonsu*, without regard to her gender. Abena's eyebrows pulled together in confusion, but I was sure she would soon come to appreciate what we conferred on her. But she continued her bright smile.

When we reached the older quarter, her smile dimmed somewhat as the streets were darker and narrower. *Oh, Abena. You do not know the contrasts of your new home. They are perhaps not so sinister or deep as when I arrived, but they are still there.*

There were still pockets of Thyenn Sharr's followers in the city, and it was slow work changing the laws regarding the Cursed. We didn't conjure a replacement name for them yet. Some nights Arlan and I tossed words back and forth to find the right one.

We arrived at my house where Edemar greeted me. "Welcome, *Yonsu*." I watched the new ambassador as she took in the huge atrium like her own but different. *Yes. We have these spaces, to see where the enemy comes.* But I hoped that Abena would be no enemy.

"Is the daymeal ready?" I asked Edemar.

"Yes, *Yonsu*. In the garden as you ordered."

"Thank you, *Rasee Yinsi*. Please tell, *Yonsa* Arlan we are here."

"Very good, *Yonsu*."

We walked through the house to get to the garden. We had repaired much of the damage, but it was still a work in progress. The ambassador stared at the scoring on the walls that wood pastes could not rub out but was too polite to ask about them. Good.

Tolen saw us and bowed. He stood to one side so I could inspect the bed of impatiens and spiky stars he worked on. The ambassador moved next to me.

"How beautiful," she said. "What is that flower?" She pointed to a patch of spiky stars.

"It's an indigenous plant."

"It's lovely," she said.

"You have done a wonderful job restoring the gardens, Tolen," said Irdrana.

"Restoring?" interrupted the Ambassador.

"Yes," I replied. "During the upset, followers of the Faith Progressive Church caused a great deal of trouble."

"Thank you, Ambassador Vos," said Tolen. "*Yonsu* Klath has been an immense help. I am old and turning soil takes strong arms."

She smiled at me. "This is why you've turned down dinners at my house?"

"I do admit I have become quite the homebody," I said. We both noticed the new ambassador watching us with interest, trying to figure out what we were to each other.

There would be time enough for Abena to learn of the close ties to the major houses of Ostakis.

A housemaid brought glasses of wine.

"Ambassador," I said. "I warn you that the wine of House Klath is much stronger than Earth wine."

"Yes," laughed Seyatt, "the last ambassador made himself the fool with it."

Irdrana shot him one of her famous dagger-eyed looks. Seyatt grimaced, then smiled again charmingly at the new ambassador. From the silly grin on his face, he seemed quite taken with Abena Kamali.

Poor woman.

Arlan walked into the garden with little Aulkus over his shoulder.

"Dadda!" said Aulkus, holding out his arms in supplication.

"I'm sorry, Kaj," he breathed, so no one else heard. "He's been fussing for you all morning."

I took the boy who clung to me, but I caught the subtle shift in my partner's scent that put off little Aulkus.

"You must let Ija take him for a couple of days," I whispered.

Arlan blushed. "I know. I wish you didn't have to do this now."

"It's just the daymeal. Be patient, love. I have no other business today I can't put off."

Irdrana cleared her throat. "Trademaster Klath."

"Sorry. Domestic issues. Ambassador Kamali, let me introduce my partner Arlan Klath and our son, Aulkus."

Abena smiled, though her eyes betrayed curiosity. But then again, she had many things about which to wonder.

I let Aulkus sit on my lap as the servants served daymeal. It was entirely unconventional to allow a child to do so, and Abena's eyes were question marks the entire time. Aulkus made a thorough mess of the meal, and my clothes, but I only laughed.

"He has your eyes," said Abena.

I looked into Aulkus' eyes. And though they were blue like mine, they carried his papa's shape and had the crystal shards of gold wound through them. They were quite startling.

"No, he has my partner's more, I think."

"Partner's?" said Abena, now thoroughly confused.

"Yes. You see here on Ostakis a third gender carries the reproductive parts of both. Arlan is one such individual."

Abena blinked, and I wondered if she was a fool. "How did Ostakians evolve this third gender?"

"They didn't. The first colonists interbred with the indigenous people here, who are all inter-sexed. The genetic heritage of those people is now a part of humans on Ostakis."

Abena's mouth formed a wide *o*, which was un-ambassadorial, but she recovered herself quickly.

"This information was not in my briefing packet."

I nodded. "Unfortunately, powerful members of the first greeting committee withheld that information. We are sharing it with you freely, so we do not repeat the mistakes of the past. I would, however, ask that you learn more about Ostakis before you make your reports."

"Yes. Earth almost didn't send another ambassador. Ostakis has a terrible reputation with Earth visitors."

This was a lie though, one to make a point. I knew that Abena was on the ship that followed the first contact teams. She, however, did not know I knew.

With a little nod of my head, I acknowledged her words. "We do not deny that. But the political climate has changed somewhat, and the unrest that disturbed Earth relations has calmed down."

"I am pleased. But tell me Trademaster Klath, what happened to our Ambassador Kaj Deder?"

"Unfortunately, he got lost in the desert during the unrest."

This was true enough. I came out of the desert a different man.

"Is there no way to find him? We'd like, at least, to send his body home."

I glanced at my son and my partner both of whom I loved more than life itself.

"I assure you, Ambassador Kamali. He is home."

Glossary

Main Characters

Kaj Deder—Earth—Earth Ambassador

Arlan Klath—Ostakis—Accountant House Klath

Thyenn Sharr—Ostakis—High Priest

Secondary Characters

Aulkus Klath—Ostakis—Trademaster Ostakis

Pib Alluvem—Ostakis—Part-time Accountant

Irdrana Vos—Ostakis—Ostakis Ambassador, Planetary Liason

Mar Seyatt—Ostakis—Mayor of Kiji Ost

Places

Kiji Ost—Largest city-state of Ostakis

Kiji Amst—Second largest Ostakian city state

Lake Veller—Northern point of Kiji Ost

Church Point District—At the edges of Lake Veller and location of the Faith Progressive Church Cathedral

Dastoan Heights District—Where House Klath is located. Sandwiched between Church Point District and the Garden District.

Garden District—Where Kaj's assigned residence is located, north and east of central downtown Kiji Ost.

Ostakian Words

Kiji—town or city

Rasee—House

Sid-Yonsu—Son of the master (yonsu) of the house.

Yansi—Housekeeper (female)

Yinsee—House manager (like a butler) (male)

Syad—Honorific that Cursed (bi-gen) individuals use. Cursed individuals are never referred to as *yonsu* though they may gain the title *yonsa* if partnered. In Aboriginal Ostakian it means "taking a mate."

Yonsu—In Ostakian English, "master." In aboriginal Ostakian "seeking a mate." Applies to most men in a social context.

Yonsa—In Ostakian English, "mistress," though it applies to a bi-gen partner of a *yonsu*, too.

Acknowledgements

Words can't express my gratitude to Robyn Stuart, Beta reader, and best cheerleader. Your advice and encouragement helped to bring this story to life. I'll be there when you are ready to launch your book. Also thanks to writer friends, S. D, W.N, G. A., and J.W. for reading chapters and providing feedback.

Many thanks to Raevyn, Stacey Jo, and the staff of Nine Star Press whose hard work brought Ostakis to press.

About the Author

Born in a century far less progressive than how her brain is wired, Angelica engages in occupations now considered now less than reputable, one of them being a ghostwriter of erotic and romance fiction. Since time travel is not an option, in her off time she contents herself with writing about people and places in a far distant future with the twists that only come with traveling to the stars.

Angelica lives in Connecticut with an odd assortment of cats and humans and putters at hobbies ranging from art to bird watching when she's not turning a phrase for her supper.

Email: angelica@missprimm.com

Facebook: www.facebook.com/MissPrimmWriter

Twitter: @MissPrimm

Instagram: www.instagram.com/angelica_primm

Website: www.missprimm.com

Also Available from NineStar Press

Connect with NineStar Press

Website: NineStarPress.com

Facebook: NineStarPress

Facebook Reader Group: NineStarNiche

Twitter: @ninestarpress

Tumblr: NineStarPress